REA

DO NOT REMOVE
CARDS FROM POCKET

Published by Hells Canyon Publishing, Inc., Halfway, Oregon.
First printing, 1994

Publisher's Cataloging in Publication Data

Beam, Joan
    Emily Louise / Joan Beam. Halfway, Or. :
Hells Canyon Pub., c1994. 1st ed.
    p.   cm.

    ISBN 0-9633919-8-4

Library of Congress Catalog Card No.: 93-79445

Printed in the United States of America

First Edition

Cover design by Steve Lawrie

Emily Louise

Joan Darlington Beam

EMILY LOUISE
CHAPTER 1

Alone in a small, square room Miss Theresa Freidmann lay, twisted and tiny on the high, white bed. She frowned, her eyes fixed on the open transom above the door and her frown deepened as once again she heard the voice in the hallway. It was a new voice, Miss Freidmann was sure of that. The voice of a stranger.

With slow, painful movements, she tried to move higher in the bed, but her body clung to the pillows propped behind her back. Only her head and neck bent forward awkwardly as she peered, listening intently, toward the door.

Miss Freidmann need not have gazed at the drab, brown door. From her half sitting position, she could have looked from the window of the room. She could have looked down on the snowy streets of Saskatoon, Saskatchewan in mid-winter of 1945. And if she had looked, she might have noticed that those who walked the streets below walked swiftly, shoulders hunched against the biting prairie wind. No one paused to glance at the gold-lettered door of Saint Anne's Home for the Chronically Ill and the Aged.

Miss Freidmann, however, did not care to look out the window. For five long years, her view had been limited by its oblong dimensions. Five years, and the scene was as unchanged as the heavy green curtains that steadfastly framed the sides. Only Miss Freidmann had changed. As the arthritis had clutched and torn at her limbs, so the pain and desperation had clutched and torn at her spirit. And now, although she was only twenty-nine, she was a woman old and crotchety, grotesquely deformed and irritatingly pathetic.

Now, she never concerned herself with the life scurrying past on the street below. Beyond the window was a day, cold or warm, fine or stormy. In any event, a day that had to be endured and, therefore, a day to be complained about. Miss Freidmann ignored the window and ignored the day. The door had opened abruptly and she gave her attention to the white-clad figure who entered with arrogant assurance.

It was, as she had feared, a new girl.

"Time to wash up," the girl said. She set an enamelled basin of water on the bedside table and groped in the stand for a towel.

Miss Freidmann watched her in dismay. She didn't like new girls. She didn't like new anything. She wanted only routine. Comfortable routine, unchanged and unbroken.

The new girl was well-built, almost plump. As she bent over, the white uniform tightened over rounded hips and opened about her neck, hinting at breasts that were full, firm, and mature. Miss Freidmann noted these things and cared little. And she noted also, that if the body was that of a woman, the face was that of a girl. Round, flushed red, and dotted with freckles. It was a laughing face. Not at all pretty. Miss Freidmann didn't trust it. She never trusted any face that laughed. Furthermore, the girl had scandalously red hair and she couldn't be more than a day over twenty. Too young to know how to handle crippled limbs.

Whining a bit, Miss Freidmann said, "Sister Mary Sophia always washes my face and hands for me."

"Does she, then?" The voice was mocking. "Well, Sister Mary Sophia is a saint and Emily Louise is a sinner. An out-and-out sinner. So this day, I'm thinking, you'll be washing your face and hands for yourself."

Miss Freidmann trembled and looked hopefully toward the door. If only Sister Mary Sophia would come. Sister Mary Sophia with the soft voice and gently swishing robes, the tender compassion in her hands. "My fingers," she murmured, raising with an effort the gnarled, twisted, hands. "You'll have to help me wash." And then, irritably, "Who are you?"

"Emily Louise is the name. Irish and Scotch. A bit of a mixture you might say. But then, nearly everyone in

Canada is a mixture. A hodge-podge from the mixing bowl, so we are."

The eyebrows were red, too, and raised quizzically.

"And you are Miss Theresa Freidmann, aged twenty-nine, and you've been here five years. See, I know all about you. I read it on your chart. And I said to myself, right then and there, 'Emily Louise, my girl, there, with a name like that, is a mixture to beat your own.' Theresa Freidmann. A name such as that and no religion at all. For shame." The voice was mocking again. "You have to be something, you know. Otherwise, you're nothing at all. That's what my mother always says. Mother is the Irish half. A good Catholic and very devout. And there she is married to a great big Scotsman. But he's gentle mind you, gentle as a kitten, only a little odd, being a Presbyterian and all."

Emily Louise pushed the stand a little closer to the bed. "Now, you get your patties in this nice warm water and limber your fingers a bit and be getting yourself nice and presentable for supper. Ah, there's an occasion now. Supper at Saint Anne's. I'll bet you can hardly wait."

Hardly wait, indeed. Miss Freidmann could tell this Emily Louise . . . However, Emily Louise had already gone. The door was closed and the steady footsteps were fading up the corridor.

Supper at Saint Anne's an occasion? It was Friday, wasn't it? There'd be fish. Every Friday there was fish. Miss Freidmann had washed her hands before she remembered she could never hold the soap. She wouldn't wash her face though, no matter what that girl said. She couldn't wring out the wash cloth. If only Sister Mary Sophia would come.

Sister Mary Sophia didn't come. Only Emily Louise came back and she took the bowl away without washing Miss Freidmann's face. "Now brush your hair and make yourself beautiful," she urged.

"Aren't you going to help me?" Miss Freidmann didn't have time to whine. The girl was almost out of the door.

"Sure now, and why should I be helping you to brush

your hair, when up the hall old Thompson has just wet his bed. At least, I hope it's only wet and nothing worse. And in Fourteen there's some poor soul sitting up and spitting blood all over the place. Brush your own hair, my girl. Emily Louise has other things to do."

Alone and desperate, Miss Freidmann reached for the buzzer, but it had fallen beside the bed. In vain, she tried to turn and stretch her arms. Her limbs had been bent and still for too long. If she could have just reached the buzzer, she could have called Sister Mary Sophia. Tears stinging her eyes, she let her head fall back against the unfluffed pillows. She'd tell Sister Mary Sophia when she did come.

However, the door didn't open. Only the wind came and fussed coldly against the window pane.

Supper, when the blue clad girl from the kitchen brought it in, was not fish. It was worse. It was an omelette. Miss Freidmann put the metal cover back over the plate and tried to forget it was there. The cook at Saint Anne's had a passion for cutting an onion into an omelette. And Miss Freidmann had learned never to trust an egg that battled for flavor with an onion. She nibbled a piece of bread and butter and suspected that it wasn't butter at all, only margarine. And as she nibbled, she pondered on how Sister Mary Sophia could keep her serene faith in the face of hundreds of Fridays and hundreds of platters of fish and omelettes.

For dessert, there was red jello. Miss Freidmann couldn't eat the red jello either. Who was the man in Fourteen? And what would cause him to spit blood all over the place? For that matter, where was room Fourteen? For five years, Miss Freidmann's pain-filled world had been bound by the four walls of room number Two. Life beyond it was a mystery. She was not grateful to Emily Louise for opening the doors on a mystery. Slowly, she sipped her tea. All she had eaten from the tray had been the bread and butter and a piece of sponge cake. She hadn't liked the sponge cake very well, either.

The girl in blue came back for the tray. Saint Anne's was

full of girls in blue. They swept the floors and dusted the window ledges. They brought the food and took it away. And sometimes they could be prevailed upon to shut a window or pull down the shades.

This evening the girl in blue was pleasant. She smiled when Miss Freidmann asked her to turn on the overhead light, and she pulled the curtains forward, pausing a moment to look down on the bleak scene below. Apparently, it didn't look bleak to her. "I've got a date to go skating tonight," she volunteered. Her eyes were young and eager.

Miss Freidmann said, "Oh," and knew the girl was much too young to be going out with boys. But, since the war, girls did all manner of things they were too young for. While she lay there thinking of something to say, the girl with the eager eyes picked up the tray and took it away. Miss Freidmann had forgotten to have her replace the buzzer.

She was left quite alone until eight o'clock. When someone did come, it was Emily Louise, and Emily Louise was in a hurry.

"Come along, Dearie. Lift up your bottom. It's time I was finished for the day. And what a day! Believe me, this night, I'll be ready for the downy."

Miss Freidmann flinched. "It's cold. Why didn't you warm it? Sister Mary Sophia always warms it."

"I've told you before, Sister Mary Sophia is a saint and you'll get no saintly treatment from me." The freckles danced on the upturned nose. "Perhaps the cold will shock you into greater efforts. Hurry up, now. It's late and I have my bed to spray tonight, too."

Miss Freidmann bit her lips, determined to maintain her dignity. Or at least all the dignity she could hope to maintain in such a situation. The girl was rude. Downright rude. "Why do you have to spray your bed?" she asked and knew she only asked to gain time. The cold did not spur her on, it repelled. And Miss Freidmann knew little could be expected from the scant ministrations of the night attendant. Opportunity would be a long time coming willingly again.

"Bedbugs."

"Bedbugs?"

"Bedbugs." Emily Louise's voice was resigned. "Hundreds upon hundreds of the little creeping devils with a bite as wicked as the Old Man himself."

"How could there be bedbugs in a hospital?"

"Saint Anne's annex, graciously turned over to the help, is old, my Pretty. The help come and go. But the bugs stay on. For years and years, they've been hiding in the cracks and in the walls, just waiting for the tender flesh of Emily Louise." She rolled back her sleeve and showed the red welts on her arm. "There's cockroaches in the kitchen, too, so look out for the raisins in the rice pudding."

Emily Louise lifted the covers over Miss Freidmann's bent knees. She lowered her head and peered under the sheet. "What? Haven't you done anything yet? Come along. I can't wait all night. Tinkle, tinkle, Dearie. I'll go and run the water. There's nothing like the sound of running water. There's an old fellow over in B-ward, right next to the bathroom. He wets his bed every time someone takes a shower. I worked there all last month and it's glad I was to get moved here. They're all nuts over there."

"Nuts?" Miss Freidmann questioned, and wished the girl would stop chattering and leave her alone for a few moments.

"Mad, Dearie. Oh, not that you ever say it out loud, mind you. They are the upper class nuts. The ones whose families can afford to pay for the attention, but think they can't afford the disgrace of sending them to the asylum. Here, they are called senile. Sounds better. But call them what they like, they're still mad. There's one old boy who wanders about stark naked. Can't keep a stitch on him. Have you ever seen a naked man?" Miss Freidmann managed, very quickly, to shake her head.

"No. You wouldn't have. Well, I don't think man's naked body was ever meant to see the light of day. If you ask me,

Adam needed those fig leaves a whole lot more than Eve. And then there's old Brandt. Take him in something to eat that he doesn't like and he pitches it at you, plate and all. I'll never forget the day I took him in a bowl of beef stew. He hates beef stew. Finished? I told you the running water would do it. Nearly always does."

Miss Freidmann nodded and found her sympathies were all with old Mr. What's-His-Name who threw bowls of beef stew. She was about to tell the girl so, but before she had time, Emily Louise had draped a little white cloth over the metal object she had removed from the bed, and holding it a good arm's length beyond the upturned nose, had disappeared into the bathroom across the hall.

Sister Mary Sophia's approach was lost amid the clatter of banging metal and running water. She was bent over the bed like a hovering angel before Miss Freidmann realized she was there. Not that Miss Freidmann put much belief in angels. However, if there were any angels, in Heaven or anywhere else, then they would be exactly like Sister Mary Sophia. She almost sobbed. "I've missed you, Sister. I haven't seen you all afternoon."

"I know, my Dear," the voice was soft and the sure hand smoothing and fluffing the pillows.

"My hands hurt and my back aches. I'm going to need a pill."

"Of course, my Dear. I have it here."

Gratefully, Miss Freidmann swallowed the little white pill. "My toes hurt, Sister, and my fingers."

"Yes, I know," the voice soothed. "It's very painful." Sister Mary Sophia had straightened the covers and was at the door. "I'll say a little prayer for you," she said and smiled as she left the room.

Miss Freidmann closed her eyes. Quietly, she lay in the darkness and waited for the relief. And in that moment when the last pain-filled limb floated free from her body, Miss Freidmann saw a vision.

She saw a man. He was very old and very bony and quite naked. He was running down the corridor trying to catch a fig leaf. Miss Freidmann could hardly resist a snicker. Then she noticed there was something very odd about the fig leaf. It had a face. The face was dotted with freckles and every time the naked old man reached to pick up the fig leaf, it laughed and danced away.

The fig leaf reminded Miss Freidmann of something she had quite forgotten. Tomorrow, she would tell Sister Mary Sophia. Tomorrow she would tell her about that new girl, Emily Louise.

CHAPTER 2

Saturday came and went and Miss Freidmann did not tell Sister Mary Sophia about the shortcomings of Emily Louise. The reason for that was quite simple. She didn't see Sister Mary Sophia.

Now, stiff, flat, and uncomfortable, Miss Freidmann lay waiting for her Sunday breakfast. Breakfast which would be late because it was Sunday and the entire staff deserted to the chapel. Of course, it would be a better breakfast, hot rolls and a little sausage. There was some comfort in that. Still waiting, she tried to move a stiffened limb, winced with the pain, and went back to her thoughts of yesterday.

Miss Freidmann had plenty of time for thinking, although yesterday hadn't given her a great deal to think about. Early in the morning, determined to report the brashness of the new girl, she had asked for Sister Mary Sophia. She had been told that Sister Mary Sophia was much too busy to come and see anyone because she was still attending the patient in room Fourteen.

"You don't mean she is still in there looking after that old man?" Miss Freidmann asked.

And Emily Louise had replied, "Sure and that's exactly where she is. He got much weaker during the night. He doesn't even sit up to spit anymore. He just lays there, letting it ooze out of the side of his mouth like. Sister Mary Sophia sits beside him, wiping it off and holding his hand and praying. I'll tell you, she's a saint, so she is. And we, neither one of us, would want to be disturbing a saint, now would we? So you just keep your little pinkies away from that buzzer, Dearie. I'll be back as soon as I have time."

Time for Emily Louise had apparently been scarce. Her attentions were limited to the barest necessities and it was well into the afternoon before she appeared briefly at Miss Freidmann's bedside to straighten the covers and rub her back. And Miss Freidmann, mindful of how the most ordinary conversations seemed to end in room Fourteen, considered carefully and then asked about the bedbugs. So, for the first time, she came to hear of Sister Mary Phillipe.

"You mean you don't know Sister Mary Phillipe?" Emily Louise asked. "You don't know what you're missing, Dearie. She's in charge of the cleaning and she's very thorough. When you first see her, she looks a little odd. All thin and bent in her black robes. And a little sharp face. Almost like a witch, you might say. She heard me last night with the sprayer, and with never a knock, into my room she came. Me with the floor not swept and the air thick with mist. Says I to myself, 'Emily Louise, my girl, you're in for it.' But what did she do? Well, I'll tell you, she's not at all witch-like when you see the eyes of her, all pinched up and sparkling. 'Emily Louise,' she says, 'You're a girl after my own heart. You'll never know the trouble I have getting the help to spray their beds. Bless you,' she says. And there she was, down on her hands and knees, getting fluff all over her robes and spraying the floor and the cracks.

Emily Louise chuckled at the memory and rubbed, much too vigorously, up and down Miss Freidmann's back. "Sister Mary Phillipe is a smart one all right," she continued. "When she lifted my mattress to spray the bed springs, there was my new love story book underneath. But she pretended not to notice, seeing she's renounced such worldly things. She kept her eyes on the bedbugs and every time she saw a dead one, she said a "Praise Be To God" and sprayed a little harder. And there we were, both of us, the tears streaming from our eyes and wee brown varmints kicking their last on the floor." She finished, ruefully, "But we never got them all. I got another bite."

Miss Freidmann was recalled from her reveries of Emily Louise and the bedbugs by the sight of a spider crawling up the wall. It was a little brown spider. Miss Freidmann couldn't keep her eyes from it. She watched as it went higher and higher and she could have sobbed when she realized that if it tumbled onto her bed, she wouldn't be able to reach out and brush it away.

A girl in blue came at last with the breakfast tray. She began to wind up the bed slowly because Miss Freidmann's body stiffened during the night. Getting wound up for breakfast was Miss Freidmann's first effort of the day. Long ago, she had given up all attempts at bravery.

In the midst of the process, Emily Louise appeared. She stood in the doorway watching as, inch by inch, the bed went higher. When Miss Freidmann was finally settled, she said, "Sister Mary Sophia sent me to ask if you will be wanting an enema this morning. And it's not happy I am to be asking. 'Sister,' I says, 'You wouldn't want me to go walking down the hall with the enema can on the Holy Sabbath. And me with a clean uniform on and all?' But she said I was to ask, seeing you didn't get any extra attention yesterday. So, it's asking I am." She added, hopefully, "There's some new pills. Little brown ones. I could bring you a couple tonight, instead. Old Bob, the orderly, says they're awful good."

Miss Freidmann carefully worked her crooked fingers and lifted the cover form the plate. Sausages. Four of them. There were usually only three. Sausages, enemas, and little brown pills. "Would you be giving me the enema?" she asked.

The green eyes gazed toward the ceiling. "Indeed I would, with Sister Mary Sophia busy in Fourteen with . . ."

"I'll take the pills," Miss Freidmann answered quickly. Enemas and brown pills with her breakfast, yes. But that old man in Fourteen, no. She was quite unprepared for the gratitude.

"You will? Well, bless your heart. If there's one thing I hate, it's the enema can. You're a dear, kind soul and I'll tell you what I'll do. I'll hurry and make the rounds, then I'll come back and give you a nice bath. From top to toe. Clean sheets and all." Emily Louise fluffed the pillows behind Miss Freidmann's head and poured the coffee cream over the cereal she never ate. "Believe me," she said, "I'll give you the best bath you ever had in your life."

Miss Freidmann ate her breakfast and waited with what scant courage she could muster. She did not look forward to a bath at the hands of Emily Louise. That girl moved far too fast and crippled limbs moved painfully slow.

True to her word, Emily Louise appeared carrying a basin of water, the clean linens tucked under her arm. Miss Freidmann assessed them expertly and her spirits sank still lower. There were two sheets. She contemplated the movements necessary for changing a bottom sheet. Movements to be superintended, apparently, by Emily Louise. "The underneath sheet is still clean," she said hopefully.

"From top to toe, like I promised," Emily Louise answered. She removed two of the pillows and Miss Freidmann's head fell back with a little thump.

"Don't move me so fast," she squealed.

"I didn't move you. You let your head fall yourself."

"You're supposed to help me." Miss Freidmann allowed her irritation to triumph. "Now you just be more careful or I'll tell Sister Mary Sophia."

Emily Louise smiled brightly. "You needn't bother," she said. "They won't fire me, if that's what you're getting at. They can't get girls to stay here, you know. They come because it sounds glamorous, being a ward aide and all. But as soon as they find out the aide is just maid with the "M" dropped off, the excitement fades. And an eight hour day that keeps you on the go for twelve hours, with an hour or two off here and there, catch as catch can. Well, it's no picnic, Dearie. There's plenty of jobs that are better. And sweeter, if I may say so. Besides," she added confidently, "they won't fire me. I owe a bill."

Miss Freidmann opened her eyes too soon and felt the sting of the soap. "You owe a bill? Here? You look healthy enough to me." For the first time it occurred to her, "healthy" was a good word for Emily Louise.

"Oh, I'm healthy enough. It's not that." Then she said, with obvious relish, "I had a baby."

"A baby?" Miss Freidmann stared. Was that girl going to stand there without a ring on her finger and brazenly admit . . .

That was precisely what she was admitting. "Oh, so you have heard of them, have you? Well, that's what it was. A baby. You're looking at a fallen woman. Does it shock you, being bathed by a fallen woman?"

The towel was over her face so Miss Freidmann couldn't answer. For that, she was rather grateful. What was Mother Superior thinking about, having a girl like that in here?

Emily Louise turned back the sheet. "My, but you're thin, aren't you? Bony, too. Like a crooked-breasted turkey. You ought to eat more."

Ought to eat more? Miss Freidmann could not voice her thoughts. Well, it was certain Emily Louise didn't need to eat more. Her chest wasn't thin. But, she had just had a baby. "You . . . you aren't married," she accused.

"Well, I have no ring, if that's what you mean," Emily Louise agreed. "I would have had one though, if we'd just had another week." All at once her voice softened and her eyes seemed to grow dark and dreamy. "And sure, it's married we were, at that, in our hearts. That's the trouble with the Irish. They do their thinking with their hearts. And perhaps it's good they do. Otherwise, there wouldn't have been the baby. The little boy, as Irish as his daddy, with big blue eyes and curly black hair."

"Where is he?"

"Killed," Emily Louise said simply. "In one of those crazy planes he loved. They put a spell on him, so they did. He couldn't leave them alone. And in the end, they got him altogether." She gazed absently before her, her hands dangling in the basin of water.

"I meant the baby," Miss Freidmann said quickly and hoped the girl would realize she was lying there with her chest all wet and cold and quite bare.

"I gave him away." Emily Louise spoke briskly. She dabbed Miss Freidmann's chest and stomach with the towel, pressing her fingers with mock concern over every rib bone. "It's a good thing you didn't have that enema. You'd have washed right away. Now let's do your feet and legs. Your toes are a sight, you know. Have you seen them lately?"

Miss Freidmann shook her head. Of course, she hadn't seen her toes. For years, she hadn't cared to look and couldn't have seen them if she had wished. Her feet were curled well back out of sight behind the bent knees. She asked, because she couldn't understand the girl at all, "Why did you give your baby away?"

"Why?" Emily Louise looked up from the toes that were a sight, and questioned, "Why, indeed? Why give him away when every bit of me was crying for him?" Suddenly her green eyes flashed. "Let me tell you, my girl, it's not the selfish ones who give up their babies. For all the time he moved inside me and I'd light a candle to his dear daddy in Heaven, I prayed and prayed. And I knew I could never give him up. I'd face the world and I'd break my mother's heart. But, the babe was mine. Mine, do you see?"

Miss Freidmann nodded, although she didn't see at all and if that girl pushed any harder on her toes, she'd scream.

"Then, late one night, the pains came," Emily Louise continued, and her voice became almost reverent. "I went to the chapel, not knowing what to do. There I knelt, in the dark, with just the little candle flickering. And the Blessed Mother, herself, seemed to come to me. All sweet and smiling and lovely, she was. 'Emily Louise,' she said, 'You've sinned, my child. Even a sin for love is still a sin.' And She, who'd given up her own Son, told me what I had to do. 'You have to give him up,' she said. 'You alone must suffer for your sin. You cannot break your mother's heart and mark the life of the child. Let him go,' she said. 'And I promise, that wherever he goes, there love will go with him.'"

Miss Freidmann lay speechless, as Emily Louise pressed her heels much too hard against the rim of the wash basin and sloshed the water over and over her toes. And all the time her voice went on. "So, I went upstairs and when the time came, I closed my eyes and said, 'Put me to sleep, Sister, and take the baby. Quickly, before I ever see the darlin' face.' 'You must promise, Emily Louise,' she said, 'never to ask about the child.' 'I promise,' I said, and the pain came again, and that was all. So now the dear baby is bringing joy and love to someone else. Didn't the Blessed Mother, herself, tell me that where he went, there would be love?"

Miss Freidmann stared at the girl bent over her bed. "How do you know the baby was a boy?" she asked.

Emily Louise shrugged and smiled a little. "I just know. How does a woman know? But know, I do. A baby boy as Irish as his daddy. And he a man to gladden the heart of anyone. All big and strong and smiling. You see," she volunteered, "he instructed the young pilots. One day, the plane crashed. They sent his body back to his mother. I wasn't his wife and so I had no claim. Afterwards, I went and had a talk with the Padre on his station and he told me I should keep my secret in my own heart. So that's what I did, and later the Padre arranged for me to come here to Saint Anne's. So," she said, and the teasing lilt came abruptly back into her voice, "you are being washed by a fallen woman. Think of that, my Dear. Now turn over and let's have a go at your back."

"I can't turn," Miss Freidmann murmured. "You'll have to help me."

"All right, then." Emily Louise pulled the sheet completely away and Miss Freidmann's gaze encountered her own stick-like legs that seemed to end with the curve of her bent knees. Why couldn't that girl leave her covered?

"Over we go. Oops! What's this?"

"It's a sandbag, under the pillow. It helps to support my legs."

"Dear Mother. What next? A sandbag beside your legs.

I can think of better things to go to bed with."

As Emily Louise, with firm, strong movements, began to wash her back, Miss Freidmann gazed at the wall and contemplated. The girl was right. There wasn't a doubt that she could think of better things to go to bed with. This Emily Louise, who made having a baby out of wedlock seem quite natural and even, Miss Freidmann tried to banish the thought, desirable.

"There, now." Emily Louise was unfolding a crisp, white sheet. "We'll change your bed and you'll be all clean and pretty. Perhaps you'll have a caller."

"I never have callers," Miss Freidmann tried to sound unconcerned.

"What, no family? No brothers or sisters? Or a lover, perhaps, eating his heart away all these long years? Wouldn't that be romantic, now?"

"I did have a lover, his name was Alfred," Miss Freidmann answered defensively. However, she knew in her heart that Emily Louise would never have considered her affair with Alfred an affair of love. "We were almost engaged. Don't roll me like that. You're hurting my back."

"If you expect to get the bed changed, you'll have to roll over the hump. What happened to Alfie?"

"So many things happened," Miss Freidmann said, allowing the self pity to creep into her voice. "Mama died and less than two months later, Papa had a heart attack and he died, too. At the same time, my joints started swelling and I became very ill. I don't remember much about anything after that. I was in the general hospital for several months and then they brought me here to Saint Anne's. Ooh, you've got my heel caught. Stop it. You're hurting my foot."

"Bless your bones," Emily Louise said irreverently. "Your joints stick out every which way. It's impossible to roll you without getting you hung up somewhere. You still haven't told me what happened to Alfie."

"Alfred went to England with the army," Miss Freidmann said carefully. "He married a girl from London and I haven't heard what happened to him after that."

"I should think not. Let his wife worry about what happened to him after that. Cast your eyes about for another, my Pretty. Although there's not much of a selection here. Still, there's old Bob, the orderly. You might make a try for him." Then she said, soothingly, "Weren't Mama and Papa a bit young to die?"

"Mama was. She'd never been very well. Papa was nearly seventy. He came from Germany and met and married Mama in Montreal. Mama was French Canadian. She was very pretty."

"And a good Catholic, no doubt?"

"She was before they were married. You see, Papa was . . ." she hesitated. "Papa made a lot of money. He was very good to Mama and he said they agreed, when they were married, never to let religion come between them."

"And Papa stayed away from the synagogue, too, I suppose?"

"Yes, he did." The girl was shrewd, but there was no scorn. Miss Freidmann felt a little defensive about Papa Freidmann and the Jews.

"And you stayed away from both?"

Really, it was none of the girl's business. Still, no one asked Miss Freidmann about her family anymore. "Mama and Papa both said I should choose for myself," she explained.

"So you ended up choosing neither," Emily Louise put in. "Well, Dearie, they both believed in something. And they took care of their own souls at any rate. So, if I were you," she said cheerfully, "I'd be doing some serious thinking about my own. You never know when it's your turn to go. Now in our family, we did it differently. Father said Mother could take me to Mass with all the beads and folderol if she liked, but Jamie would have to take his religion like a man. We all argued about it for six days a week. Then, on Sunday morning, Father drove us to Mass, kissed Mother goodbye at the door, and he and Jamie went on to the kirk down the street."

Emily Louise took a rosary from her pocket and held it up, lovingly. "I could never manage without the beads, myself," she said softly. "I guess I'm like my mother. She always said she could never go into a church and pray if there wasn't a woman to talk to. You really ought to do some thinking about your soul, Dearie. Still, if you are here, it won't be too bad. Sister Mary Sophia never lets anyone die without getting them baptized. That's something."

Miss Freidmann turned her head sharply. Surely this girl wasn't implying that she was going to die here. And almost as though it might be at any minute. Miss Freidmann thought of the man in Fourteen and shuddered.

Emily Louise, busily brushing her hair, paused in midstroke. "What's the matter? Did I pull a bit? If you ask me, you need a hair cut and a rinse. Certainly a rinse. Look at all these gray hairs. And I'll bet your hair used to be thick and black like Mama's. Yes, you must look like Mama. Only you're not pretty. Too thin." She picked up the basin of water and turning to leave, said casually, "I'll buy you a hair dye next time I'm downtown, if you want me to."

Hair dye! Miss Freidmann gasped. She certainly was not going to dye her hair. Emily Louise had left and forgotten to push her bed back against the wall. She was rolled up high and from where she sat, she could see her reflection in the mirror of the dresser. Miss Freidmann gazed at her own face critically. Emily Louise was right. She wasn't as pretty as Mama. Her hair was going gray, quite gray, and she looked old. Miss Freidmann thought again of the man in Fourteen. How old did you get to look before you died? Or did, perhaps, your turn come young, like Emily Louise's lover?

Miss Freidmann pressed her thumb upon the buzzer and when Emily Louise came in, she told her, quite irritably, to get the bed pushed back against the wall.

Emily Louise was cheerful as she carried the soiled linens from Miss Freidmann's room. Room Two was one of the better rooms on the floor. To be truthful, the old girl was a bit grumpy and took an age to move around in the bed. However, the linens from her room could be dispatched down the laundry chute without any pre-rinsing. She hummed as the linens disappeared with a gentle swish. Emily Louise was inclined to judge the patients of Saint Anne's by the condition of their sheets.

She made her way to the other end of the corridor and entered room Twenty-two. Inside, sitting on the floor with her back to the door, a girl fussed jerkily with a towel. "Hello, Maribel. Did you wash your baby?"

The girl turned, then hung her head and laughed with a deep, throaty gurgle. Tenderly, despite the jerkiness of her hands, she arranged a rag doll, dripping wet, on the radiator. Maribel, at seventeen, was overly fat and mature. Her teeth were sharpened, yellow jags in her open mouth and she wore a thick bib over her cotton dress because she drooled constantly. The girl was described on her chart as a congenital syphilitic, a description that had immediately sent Emily Louise to the dictionary.

Thereafter, Maribel aroused a strange sort of pity in Emily Louise. A pity of which she was somehow ashamed. Once, not too many years ago, she and her brother, Jamie, had caught a three-legged gopher in a trap. They had kept it as a pet. She remembered the bewildered way it had tried to scratch its way to freedom with its one front leg. Emily Louise had felt exactly the same kind of pity for the gopher.

Bending over, she took the girl's hand. "You've been such a good girl, Maribel," she said, "I have a treat for you. I'm going to let you dust the hall."

The girl came to her feet, but her answer, if it was an answer, died in a grunting rumble deep in her throat. The effort seemed to make her drool even more. Head down, eyes bulging, she tried awkwardly to skip as she followed Emily Louise down the hall.

"There. Isn't that a nice dust mop now." Emily Louise had taken a brown string mop from the closet.

Eagerly, Maribel reached for the handle. She lifted it and rubbed the soft brown strings against her cheeks. For a moment, she stroked it tenderly, then in short, jerky movements, she began pushing it up and down the hall.

Maribel had a bit of Indian blood in her, enough for the Canadian government to send a check every month for her support. And sometime, a long time ago, someone had loved her. Or at least, had cared enough to give her a name like Maribel. Now, no one cared. No one at all.

Emily Louise allowed herself a moment's reflection. It was a dreary place, Saint Anne's. And if it weren't for her debt, she would be packing her bags. But, perhaps, she thought, working at Saint Anne's was part of her penance.

Curiously, she glanced at a thin and fortyish man who was coming rapidly up the stairs. Few visitors came to Saint Anne's. And visitor he certainly was, the church workers all took the elevator. She wondered if he had visited the hospital before. He sidled around Maribel and the erratic dust mop and in the process, dropped his hat. Quickly, he stooped to pick it up. However, Maribel had it first. With unbelievable dexterity, she scooped it up on the end of the mop and stood surveying it with delight. Then, letting the mop fall to the floor, she took the hat in both hands and clamped it down on her head.

Emily Louise felt a little panic as she hurried down the corridor. By the time she reached the scene, Maribel had the hat forced well down over her ears and stood, gurgling her satisfaction. The visitor stood with his hand out-stretched for his hat. Maribel ignored it completely. Head down and drooling, she stepped back, just out of his reach.

"Maribel," Emily Louise said sternly, "give the gentleman his hat. Give it to him now or I'll take away your nice mop. You wouldn't like me to do that, would you?"

Maribel looked at the mop Emily Louise had taken up in her hand. Her eyes widened as the choice seemed to reach her sleeping mind. Reluctantly, she stepped forward and allowed Emily Louise to remove the hat from her dark head.

"Begging your pardon, Sir," Emily Louise smiled as she returned the hat. "She's a bit kittenish today."

"Yes," he said. "Yes, of course." Nervously putting the crease back in his hat, he turned and hurried down the hall.

Emily Louise watched him as he continued down the corridor. "He skitters," she confided softly to the drooling Maribel, "like a scared rabbit in the green-feed. Now, get on with your dusting while I stay right here and keep an eye on you."

Further up the hall in the diet kitchen, with her white nun's habit flowing softly about her slight figure, Sister Mary Sophia worked busily, quite unaware of the visitor. Thoughtfully, she chipped at an ice cube. A thin sliver of ice on the tongue of the old man in Fourteen would help to moisten his mouth. Although, poor creature, he was almost beyond bodily help now. And no one to care if he lived or died. Still, if God saw the sparrow . . . Sister Mary Sophia sighed. Most of the dying at Saint Anne's was done alone and unmourned.

She remembered the day, a week ago now, when Bob and Mother Superior had brought the old man upstairs. They had found him outside in the alley, looking for food in the garbage barrels. Dazed and incoherent, he had been put to bed, for no one was ever turned from the door of Saint Anne's.

Most of the time, Sister Mary Sophia never knew the financial status of her charges. Only the office records noted those who were kept for pay and those who were kept in the name of mercy. The man in Fourteen had been different. He carried no papers. Too ill to even whisper his name, he lay now, dying. Mother Superior had told the police, but still there was no hint of identity. Perhaps, before he died, there would come a fleeting moment of consciousness. It sometimes happened. Sister Mary Sophia picked up the ice chips. It was a blessing she had the help of Emily Louise. It gave her time to go back to the bedside of the old man, to sit quietly, and to pray a little more.

Sister Mary Sophia was shocked from her contemplations by the violent entrance of Emily Louise. The diet kitchen door swung wildly, seeming to catch the excitement. "Dear Mother in Heaven, Sister. You'll never guess. Miss Freidmann has a visitor. And it's a *man*."

CHAPTER 3

Emily Louise, her shoes off and a wool blanket tucked under her chin, lay on the bed in her room. A book of love stories was open in her hand. Emily Louise, however, wasn't reading. She was dreamily weaving a love story of her own.

The visitor was Miss Freidmann's Alfred, returning from the war. His wife had died and he was looking up his old love. Or his wife hadn't died and he was merely looking for an amorous interlude. The only trouble was that Miss Freidmann was in no shape for any interlude, amorous or otherwise. And the visitor was a very disappointing Alfred. Still, if he wasn't the missing Alfie, then who could he be?

Emily Louise let her gaze return to her book. The woman pictured on the cover was gossamer-clad and quite shocking. What must Sister Mary Phillipe have thought? She slipped the book back under her pillow and turned her face restlessly toward the window, wishing that Sister Mary Sophia hadn't told her to take some time off. True, she had been putting in a lot more than her eight hours lately, but Emily Louise didn't mind. And even though the patients were a depressing and a queer lot, she felt more of a kinship with them than she did with the girls in the annex.

The girls in blue occupied the rooms at the other end of the hallway. Two and three to a room, their laughter and chatter could be heard even through the closed doors. Across the hall was the room shared by Katie and Hilda. They were the only other ward aides at Saint Anne's and, by virtue of white being above blue, they kept to themselves.

Emily Louise was grateful for the tiny room she had to herself. She felt no affinity for Katie and Hilda. Hilda, blue-eyed and serious with a diamond perched respectably on her left hand, and little Katie, her interests only the boys in khaki or blue. Emily Louise was glad that Katie and Hilda worked together on the lower floor. Instinctively, she knew their companionship and confidences could be hers no longer. It was one of the things that had changed when she moved to the upper floor. They felt sorry for her. Emily Louise knew that and would have none of their pity. She smiled as she remembered the confidences exchanged with Miss Freidmann. Miss Freidmann would never feel sorry for her. She might, however, feel a little envious.

Emily Louise had loved. She had not loved strictly according to the rules. However, she had loved well. Extremely well. The memory still brought a glow. And even though the glow couldn't do much to lessen the pain, it did erase some of the bitterness from the forfeit. Miss Freidmann, bent and aged before her time, lay with nothing much to look forward to and, apparently, not much to look backward upon either. Her affair with the fickle Alfie apparently hadn't been much of an education. Besides, five years at Saint Anne's was enough to make a recluse out of anyone.

Emily Louise snuggled further under the blanket. It was cold and the wind was still blowing outside. The same wind would be sifting the snow through the stubble fields on the farm and would send the Black Angus cattle to hunch in the shelter of the straw pile. It was Sunday afternoon, so brother Jamie would be away courting his Florence. Brother Jamie, canny like a true Scot. No danger of his Florence ever ending up at a place like Saint Anne's. Emily Louise covered her head with the pillow and shut out the animated chatter of the girls down the hall. There was, after all, something to be said for the company of the bedbugs. They might nibble now and then, but they did it quietly. There was no laughing and carrying on to destroy the mood of one's reflections.

It was nearly supper time when she awakened. Supper at Saint Anne's was a little better on Sunday nights. There would be a cold plate and a salad. Miss Freidmann would be happy with the salad, even a wartime cabbage salad.

Making her way back to the main building, Emily Louise paused, undecided, on the stairs. Should she eat first and then attend to the patients on the second floor? Or should she go and see that they all had their trays before going on herself to the dining room? She decided to eat her own meal first, a decision somewhat influenced by the fact that it was considerably easier to get on to the second floor than it was to get back off it again.

When she went back up, the girls in blue had taken out the trays. Emily Louise stared, dejectedly, at the four that were left for her in the diet kitchen. She took Maribel's first. It was the easiest.

Maribel's tray had metal dishes and a single wooden spoon. Very practical, a wooden spoon, because it didn't rattle so effectively against the dishes. And if the playful Maribel cared to bend it between her teeth, the wooden spoon broke first. Maribel had a blank space in her mouth where she had first tested the possibilities of a silver teaspoon and Sister Mary Sophia could explain in great detail the agonized contortions of a Maribel with a tooth ache.

"Here you are, Maribel. Here's your nice supper. Where's your tablecloth?"

Maribel gurgled and pointed to the newspaper spread on the floor in front of the radiator.

Emily Louise put down the tray, tied a new bib around the girl's neck, and carefully hooked the door on the outside when she left. Once, Mother Superior, ushering Father Mullaine upstairs to see a sick patient, had encountered Maribel in the hall eating a sandwich put together with bologna and sponge cake. Bob had been sent upstairs with the hook for the door the very next day.

Back in the diet kitchen, Emily Louise picked up two more of the small trays. There was a single bowl and a single feeding cup on each. They were for room Eight, a room Emily Louise would have preferred to avoid. However, there was no avoiding. She pushed open the door and put both trays down on a single table between the beds. The two heads turned toward her as she tied a heavy bib under each prickly chin. Then, with a bright "Open wide my boys. Here comes your supper," she bent over the first bed. The teaspoon emptied into the toothless mouth and Mister Fred, speechless for his second year after a stroke, swallowed noisily.

Back to the table, she went, to the bread and soup mixture. "Your turn, George. Down it goes. Just like beefsteak, George. Good supper tonight."

The dark eyes burned up at her as George shook his head. But he swallowed quickly. George had once been a big man, perhaps a forceful man. Now he lay helpless as a child and as pathetically eager to cooperate.

Fate had not dealt mercifully with George. Surgeons from the University had opened and probed into his head. Skillfully, they had discovered and removed the tumor that rested upon his brain. As the months passed, the wound healed, the dark hair grew again. And that was all. Deep inside, the damage was done. Now the mind that would not move his muscles, still responded to the pangs of hunger and desire. Tonight, there was beef soup over the bread and George was grateful. And even while he shook his head at Emily Louise, he smiled his satisfaction. The bread, softened with the soup, slid down easily. It was better than the breakfast cereal which tended to lump and catch in his throat.

George was one of the few patients in Saint Anne's who was frequently visited by doctors. They came, entire classes at a time, from the University. They pinched and examined, lectured and exclaimed. And for awhile after they came, George's eyes would glow with hope again. Then, the days passed, the hope faded, and always the silence lay upon room Eight. The silence was caught and held by a framed picture on a table by George's bed. It was a photograph of a woman and a little girl, a child with long dark curls and ruffles on her dress. Across the bottom of the picture was a message, "To Daddy. With all our love." Whenever George turned and looked at the picture, his brown eyes filled with tears and without a sound, he cried. There were times when Emily Louise could not look into George's eyes.

Emily Louise turned again and went back to the bread and milk and to Mister Fred. From bed to bed she went, a spoonful into one open mouth and then into the other. Sickeningly, the food disappeared. It was always so. At every meal, Emily Louise reconsidered her decision. If she ate first, she wished she hadn't. If she didn't eat first, she didn't care to eat at all. He of the bread and milk tried to raise his arm. Shaking violently, it collided with the spoon and the mixture spilled on the bed.

"Mister Fred," Emily Louise exclaimed, "you just open your mouth and leave the rest to me. There's a good fellow now."

The man on the bed choked a little and she took the cup with the pouring spout and gave him a drink of sweetened tea. "There you are. Now, bless you. And don't go messing your bed. It's Bob's day off and I don't want to be stuck to change it." She would have to change it though, she knew. They were both wet. She didn't need to look.

Once more, she went back to the diet kitchen and picked up the remaining tray. She carried it in to Mrs. Pleoski, a gaunt and aged woman, dwarfed by the pillows that supported her. Thin, gray hair pulled back from her brow only accented the dreadful colorless gray of her skin that told, mutely, of the cancer that consumed her. At sight of Emily Louise, she began to chatter rapidly. She spoke now, only in the language she had learned in the Ukraine some eighty years ago.

Emily Louise held a feeding cup to the thin lips, but the liquid seemed only to make her cough and choke. The old woman shook her head and turned her face to the table. Emily Louise put down the cup and found an old brown pipe. She packed it with tobacco, put it between the old woman's lips, and lit a match.

Mrs. Pleoski puffed her satisfaction, the food on the tray forgotten. Emily Louise watched and waited. Left alone,

Mrs. Pleoski might have set fire to the bed and Sister Mary Sophia had decreed that the pipe was necessity. It was better than the morphine. There would be plenty of time for that later.

How much later, Emily Louise wondered? Already the disease inside the old woman was pushing and swelling in her stomach. Even now, the skin was sloughing from the protruding bones of her hips. The hospital gown lay flat over her thin chest. And beneath the gown, only twisted purple scars where once babies had suckled at her breasts.

Oblivious, the old woman puffed on in contentment, a smile about her face. She would never be like the old man in Fourteen. Even lying with death, there was a vitality to her as though death, too, was only another part of life. As though death, somehow, was just an act of living.

Emily Louise took the rosary beads from under the pillow and put them in the wrinkled hands. The flood of speech came again as Mrs. Pleoski pressed the crucifix between her palms. Taking the tray of untouched food, Emily Louise closed the door quietly and left. Perhaps, she thought ruefully, she should have stayed over in B-Ward. They were a little crazier over there, but at least they weren't so apt to die.

Sister Mary Sophia beckoned her down the hall. "I wonder, Emily Louise," she said, "if you'd come and help me change Fourteen."

"Change Fourteen?"

"Yes," Sister Mary Sophia had a voice softened by years of praying. "He's very low and his bed is wet."

"Sister," Emily Louise protested as she followed the billowing robes down the hall, "I can't. I can't lay a finger on that old man. He's nearly dead."

"Hush," Sister Mary Sophia said kindly. "We can't let him die in a wet bed. You won't mind once you get started. Death is always a little frightening at first."

Emily Louise shivered as she entered the old man's room. Fourteen was a room apart. Death was there, she sensed it, could almost feel it touch her.

Sister Mary Sophia pulled the blinds and turned on the bright overhead light. The old man lay with his head flat and still on a single pillow. The pupils were rolled back under his half open eyelids and through his open mouth, every breath was a hoarse, rattling gasp. His bony fingers, seemingly the only moving part of his body, clutched and picked at the sheet.

Emily Louise stared, wide eyed. "Dear Mother in Heaven. I can't touch that old man, Sister. He's nearly dead."

"Hush," Sister Mary Sophia said softly. "Sometimes they hear. Now, get one hand on his shoulder and the other on his hip and turn him over toward you."

Standing as far from the bed as she could, Emily Louise rolled the old man on his side. His gown felt wet and warm, yet strangely clammy, beneath her hand. There was the strong odor of urine. The man on the bed gasped a little louder and suddenly a hoarse voice croaked, "Goddam you. Get off my back."

"Yes," Sister Mary Sophia said quickly, her voice louder than usual, "we will, Mister. What is your name, Mister?" There was no answer.

She put her head close to the old man's ear. "Whose back is it?" she asked. "Whose back shall we get away from?" The old man only gasped again and spoke no more.

They pulled the clean draw sheet smooth beneath him, washed and powdered his back and Fourteen, at last, lay clean and meticulously tidy in his bed. His limbs were pulled straight and his head was settled right in the middle of the pillow. The clutching fingers were allowed to rest on the top of the white spread. Sister Mary Sophia felt for a pulse beat at the side of his neck. "I don't believe," she said thoughtfully, "that he will move anymore. We ought to have Bob place a urinal."

"It's Bob's day off."

"So it is. Well then, we'll have to do it ourselves." Sister Mary Sophia took the urinal from the stand and slipped it under the covers. She kept her eyes averted as she worked. Emily Louise watched the fumbling movements of the hand under the sheet. "I don't know if I have it in the right place," Sister Mary Sophia whispered.

"Why don't you look?"

"I suppose I'll have to."

Cautiously, Sister Mary Sophia raised the sheet and peered underneath. She maneuvered the urinal, but the alignment she sought eluded her. Matter-of-factly, she took the forceps from her pocket and carefully guided the one to the other. "You can't do this with a woman," she confided. "You just have to let them wet the bed." She added, with just the faintest hint of a smile, "A man is rather conveniently constructed." Emily Louise found herself agreeing wholeheartedly.

She took the wet sheet and gown in her hand and when she left the room, Sister Mary Sophia had taken the old man's clutching fingers in her own and was quietly beginning to pray. "Hail Mary, full of grace. The Lord is with Thee . . ."

So Emily Louise consoled herself, there would be no more wet sheets from there. No more need to disturb the old man. Sister Mary Sophia had cleansed his body and now she would pray and cleanse his soul. Cleansed and ready for death; a death that Emily Louise hoped, with all her heart and soul, would come when she was safely in her room over in the annex.

Out in the hallway, the number two was dancing noisily on the call board. Emily Louise flicked it from the board, only to have it bounce right back again. She frowned. If only Saint Anne's were a little more modern, they'd have lights instead of buzzers. One could ignore a light. She stopped at the bathroom on the way down. There was no doubt what it was that Miss Freidmann would be wanting.

Emily Louise got in the first greeting. "Well, I see number two doing a jig on the call board. You needn't worry, I won't forget you. Fingers a bit better tonight, are they?"

Miss Freidmann didn't answer. It took all of her concentration to get settled comfortably on the utility Emily Louise supplied. "A little lower," she said at last. "It's hurting my back. It would be better if you'd put some pillows behind me and get the sand bag under my knees, so I won't slip down."

"A gentleman caller this afternoon and you're still worried about getting that sandbag between your knees." Emily Louise shook her head. "I expected to see you all starry-eyed. I've been in a dither for hours wondering about that visitor. Tell me, was it Alfie?"

"No. It wasn't Alfred." Miss Freidmann spoke abruptly. That girl was a distraction. She said, trying to keep the disappointment from her voice, for it had been months, even years, since Miss Freidmann had been visited by a man, "It was a business call, or perhaps I should say, a courtesy call from my lawyer."

"On a Sunday?" Emily Louise seated herself on a chair and the red eyebrows raised skeptically. "A visit from a lawyer is bad enough any day. On a Sunday it can only mean one thing, trouble. I'll wager he's up to no good."

Miss Freidmann could scarcely contain her irritation. For the first time in years, she had been visited by a gentleman and all that girl could say was that he was up to no good. "He was just passing by," she defended, "so he stopped in to make my acquaintance. I don't see anything out of the ordinary about that."

"Just passing by, was he? Well, he's the cautious type. You can tell that just from the look of him. But, you just wait awhile. Whenever a lawyer starts to call, there's something up, somewhere. My daddy never would have one within miles of the place. He always wrote out his own agreements and things and signed them and put them in the bank. He said he didn't need to pay a lawyer a fancy price for pages and pages of whereases and wherefores." She looked at Miss Freidmann shrewdly, "I'll bet Papa didn't need lawyers."

"Papa was a man and he understood those sort of things. Ames & Bates took over my affairs when I became ill. They are a very ethical firm," Miss Freidmann said emphatically. "Mr. Bates apparently died just recently and his interest has been taken over by Mr. Dickey. That was the gentleman who called. He said he wanted to get to know his clients personally."

Emily Louise's answer was only a non-committal "Hmmmm," and Miss Freidmann continued. "After all, the only communication I've ever had with them before has been a card and a quite impossible financial statement at Christmas every year. Mr. Dickey seems like a very conscientious gentleman."

"He does, does he? Well, when a lawyer comes visiting on a Sunday, it's not his conscience that's bothering him. Remember, you are Papa's daughter and act accordingly."

"I'm finished," Miss Freidmann said abruptly. She had been looking forward to talking to someone about her caller, but that girl spoiled everything. Nevertheless, she felt bound to defend him. "Mr. Dickey seemed very kind and sympathetic. He even promised to call again with some books."

"Books first, and then roses. Just look out for him when he starts sending roses. And whatever you do, don't go telling him you sleep with a sandbag."

Miss Freidmann ignored the speech. "Ames & Bates," she said, "have rented my house very profitably all these years. And it's away in the outskirts of town, too."

"Dearie, while you've been wasting away here at Saint Anne's, there's been a war on. You could rent a chicken house as long as it had a perch. Oh well, some roses, after all, might sweeten us all up a bit. And when he sends flowers, they'll be roses. He's that type."

Emily Louise left and Miss Freidmann lay quietly thinking. Maybe she was old looking, and thin like a . . . what had the girl said? A crooked-breasted turkey? Just the same, Mr. Dickey had said he would call again. Her house was rented and her affairs were in order. Thanks to Papa's business acumen, she had income enough to pay her bills at Saint Anne's. So, there was absolutely no reason why the lawyer should call again unless he was interested in seeing her. Miss Freidmann smiled. Twenty-nine wasn't old. And gray hair could be quite attractive. Anyway, he wasn't exactly young himself. Then another thought came. Married? Perhaps he was married. Quite upset, Miss Freidmann lay and worried.

It was well after eight o'clock when her door opened and Emily Louise came again. She should, by now, have been off duty for the night. In the soft glow of the bed light, Miss Freidmann saw her face, wide-eyed and ashen. She sank into a chair by the window. "He's gone, poor devil," she said. "He's gone."

"Who's gone?"

"Fourteen."

"What do you mean, gone?" Miss Freidmann asked, feeling as though she were getting a chill.

"Dead. Dead as a door nail. Dear Mother," Emily Louise said fervently, "I hope never to see the like of that again."

"Don't come here telling me about it," Miss Freidmann gasped and knew the chills on her back meant pneumonia by morning.

"Why? Why shouldn't I tell you? Sister Mary Sophia has just gone downstairs to call the undertaker. Then she said she was going into the chapel, it being the holy Sabbath and her not getting in to pray all afternoon. She told me to stay with him until the undertakers came, but I couldn't stay there any longer. Dear Mother in Heaven. Have you ever seen anyone die?"

"No, I haven't and I don't want to hear about it."

"Well, it's awful, Dearie. Just awful. Sister Mary Sophia called me in. 'Emily Louise,' says she, 'he's gone, poor soul. He's gone. And the only thing he said was that it was an awful cold place. Let's hope that's an omen,' she says. And then she started to pray. And there we were saying the Hail Marys with those dead eyes staring up at us. Did you know people die with their eyes open? It's unnatural, so it is . . . Dead eyes staring at you like that. And Sister Mary Sophia couldn't touch him until she had prayed.

Once she had done what she could for his soul, she got back to the flesh again. I had to help her fix him up."

There was a strange, hollow tone to the girl's voice and in spite of herself, Miss Freidmann questioned, "Fix him up?" She regretted the words as soon as they were spoken.

"It did seem a bit strange, fix him up. And him being beyond fixing and all. But I'll tell you what we had to do."

"No," Miss Freidmann said quickly. "No. Don't tell me any more about it. Why don't you just go away?"

"Now you wouldn't have me go and sit all alone with that dead man, would you? Or stay in the hall with all the shadows?"

"Go away. Go anywhere. I don't want to hear about it."

Emily Louise, however, didn't go away. She sat on the edge of the chair and kept right on talking. "He died with his eyes open," she repeated. "And his mouth open, too. Sister Mary Sophia pushed on his chin with her finger and then she pulled down on his eyelids. Only one eye kept popping back open again. It's unnatural, so it is. People ought to close their eyes before they die. And then Sister Mary Sophia looks at me, she all calm and not scared a bit, 'Now,' she says, 'Emily Louise. Now, we'll roll him over and pack him.' 'Pack him?' I ask, thinking maybe we'd take him up and put him in a box. But she just got a jar of cotton and the forceps and I held him over on his side while she fixed him up so there would be no chance of an accident while he was on the undertaker's cart. Then we rolled him back and when he rolled the breath wheezed out of him, sounding just like he was alive again. Sister Mary Sophia says they do that all the time. She said it was just a reflex."

Emily Louise sighed audibly. "So there he lays," she continued, "all gray looking and strange. Sister Mary Sophia folded his hands across his chest and said that all beauty leaves the body with the departure of the soul. And sure enough, it does all right, and him not much of a beauty to start with. But, as I've told you before, Sister Mary Sophia is a saint. She pulled the sheet over him as tenderly as over a sleeping kitten. Shhh! Isn't that the elevator? It must be the undertaker." Emily Louise closed the door carefully as she went, once more, out into the darkened corridor.

In the quietness of her room, Miss Freidmann was left to lie alone. And the sleep that might have been conjured by visions of books and roses, went rolling up the corridor on the rubber wheels of the undertaker's cart. The sleep that might have been wooed by the remembrance of a man's voice, a bit squeaky, but a man's nevertheless, vanished in the sharp metallic clatter of the elevator doors.

To Miss Freidmann, wide awake in her room, and to Emily Louise, making her lonely way over to the annex, the passing of number Fourteen, unknown and unmourned, was an event that would live in their minds forever.

CHAPTER 4

Emily Louise had two days away from the patients at Saint Anne's. Two days. It would be long enough to get on the north bound bus and go home. At home, she could have gone ice skating on the pond that Jamie flooded every winter. Emily Louise had only to close her eyes to see the northern lights fingering the sky and hear the swish of skate blades over the ice. Almost, she could feel the prairie wind, cold on her face, and the frost snatching her breath and laughter and holding it in white clouds on the air.

However, Emily Louise did not go home. Instead, to Sister Mary Phillipe's delight, she scrubbed her room with single-minded determination and went again after the bedbugs. That done, she turned her attentions to herself. She shampooed her shiny red hair, then stood before the mirror, eyeing a long, rebellious strand.

"I should cut you off," she said aloud. "Always flipping and flying about you are. Or perhaps, I should tie you up in rags, the way Jamie ties up the tails of the Angus steers before he takes them to the fair. But what color of rag could I tie in you without defiling the green of the emerald? You're wanton and brazen like your owner and I should take the scissors to you, so I should." Instead, she only twisted the strands loosely about her fingers and found a measure of comfort in the memory of the carefully clipped and curled tails of the Angus steers at the fair.

Emily Louise was homesick. She wanted to go home and take her troubles to her mother. She longed to lay her head, as she had as a child, against the plump, warm breast and to join with the rich, full voice, saying familiar prayers. Only she would not go. What use to destroy a mother's faith? Or listen to her father lecture that this thing would not have happened if she had spent a little more time worrying about hellfire and damnation and a little less time playing with beads?

And they'd know, of course. Truly, she resembled her mother who always said she gained twenty pounds with every baby she bore and had to stop after two, while she could still squeeze through the kitchen door. Emily Louise scrutinized her body before the mirror. It bore all the telltale signs, the maturing of breasts and hips, the stretch marks on her skin, the folds where the flesh had once been firm and tight. Perhaps later, if she wore a good tight girdle and exercised, but for now she would have to be content. She wrote them a letter and said the work was agreeing with her, she was gaining weight.

She squandered the hours of her leisure methodically and deliberately. On the afternoon of the second day, she wandered aimlessly about the five and dime, her thoughts still stubbornly returning to her home, to Jamie and the Angus steers, to her mother and her father. Again, she remembered her father's pride and knew it was all that kept her from returning. Her mother might sob, but soon she would hold her close and whisper a prayer. But her daddy was that proud. His ideas of daughters and babies would be as stern and unrelenting as they were about everything. Like lawyers, for instance. And the thought of lawyers conjured a vision of Mr. Dickey.

Emily Louise was frankly curious about Mr. Dickey. The Irish half of her preferred the notion that Mr. Dickey's call, beginning with kindness or business or anything at all, was, nevertheless, a beginning. That it would blossom into a friendship, a romance, or an affair and would bring a spark of life to the shrunken woman in Room Two. The Scot half of her, her daddy's half, only warned curtly, "stuff and nonsense."

Impulsively, Emily Louise decided to investigate. She found the address in the telephone book. The office, she discovered, was located in a business block above a hardware store. The stairs were wide and clattery. Emily Louise found herself walking on the very edge of the boards to lessen the sound of her ascent. At the top of the stairs, the hallway stretched, long uncarpeted, bleak. A man came up the stairs, passed her, and entered the door of an optometrist. A woman and a little girl came from a dentist's office and noisily descended to the street below. No one entered the door of Ames & Bates.

Emily Louise went closer and studied the opaque glass. A card, taped to the door corrected the "Ames & Bates" to read "Ames & Dickey." There was no light glowing behind the door, so apparently the office was empty.

Still, he had told the truth at any rate. It *was* Ames & Dickey. Emily Louise allowed her Irish half to triumph. She went back to the five and dime and squandered twenty-nine cents on a black hair rinse. Then, shrugging off the cold, she stopped and went into a theater for the matinee.

Wednesday morning she was joyful to see Bob on the second floor of Saint Anne's. Bob on duty meant that she would not have to feed the men in number Eight. Bob would also lift them into the wheelchair and take them to the bathroom where his big arms would hold them in the cleansing warm water.

Bob greeted her, his ruddy face slight with smile, "Good morning, Miss Emily. You're late. Five minutes."

"So I am. But then, it's beautiful I have to make myself for these poor unfortunates. And with my face, well, beauty takes time."

"You're lucky. With mine, it's impossible." His smile was friendly, almost intimate. Back in Bob's ancestry, there was a touch of the Scandinavian. His eyes were blue and wide apart. His hair was thick and heavy, somewhere between blonde and gray. He wore his shirt with the sleeves rolled to the elbows and his arms were brawny and strong. A woman, Emily Louise decided, might find a certain satisfaction in Bob's arms. On occasion, she had found herself wishing that he weren't quite so old. Forty she guessed, probably closer to fifty. Bob had never married. And yet, there was that about Bob's arms that made Emily Louise believe they had, many times, known what it was to hold a woman.

"They're fed in Eight," he remarked. "This morning I'll give them a bath. What are you going to do with Maribel?"

"I'll do her first, while you're on the enemas. You know Maribel. She gets all excited when she hears the bath water running."

"I know Maribel," he grinned, knowingly. "You know, you will really have to look after her better. I can't have her trying to crawl into the tub with Mister Fred again."

"You should keep the door locked."

"I *had* the door locked. She crawled under the partition. You know, he could have had another stroke, then and there. What do you suppose," he asked with mock seriousness, "Sister Mary Sophia would have done if she had come in and seen Maribel trying to climb into the bath with Mister Fred?"

Emily Louise laughed with delight. "Sister Mary Sophia would have closed one eye and blinked the other, that's what she would have done. Can't you imagine what she would have been like, if she hadn't been a nun?" Emily Louise pondered her own question and, relishing the possibility, answered it with another. "If she hadn't been a saint, wouldn't she have made a glorious sinner? You should have seen her with that old man in Fourteen on Sunday when you were off duty. She had to place a urinal. And do you know what she did? She used the forceps."

"Forceps?"

"Indeed, she did. She picked it up with the forceps. She takes this pleasures-of-the-flesh thing very seriously. You know," Emily Louise repressed a smile and added a little wistfully, "when I was a little girl, I always used to think I'd like to be a nun."

Bob shook his head. "You never would have managed it, Miss Emily."

"Why? I always rather fancied I'd make a good nun. But the parish priest discouraged me. He just looked at me and said he didn't think I'd have the temperament. You'd be surprised, though. I can be very submissive when I like."

Bob laughed and accused, "But you'd never think of using the forceps."

"Well, it did seem a bit awkward like. And awful cold, too."

"Miss Emily," Bob said, "if you'd entered the Holy Orders, you'd have shook the church of Rome all the way to Saint Peter's."

He left with the enema tray, a smile on his lips, and Emily Louise suspected, a story in his mind to perk up the two speechless ones in Eight. She fetched Maribel and put the girl, rag doll and all, into the bath tub.

Maribel loved the tub. She blubbered and drooled in the water, cupped her hands and poured it in little streams over her body. And when Emily Louise gently whisked the bath brush across her back, her voice changed to a gurgle and she swayed, back and forth, leaning against the strokes of the brush. Out of the tub, she stood, quite naked, carefully examining one of her breasts while Emily Louise toweled her lower limbs. Sister Mary Sophia, wearing her black street robes, peered cautiously around the door. "I'm going into town for awhile with Mother Superior. I think you and Bob will be able to manage until I get back. Perhaps," she confided, "we will be able to get some more linens."

Emily Louise nodded sympathetically. If Sister Mary Sophia had one other goal in life besides preparing her soul for Heaven, it was the acquisition of more linens for the second floor of Saint Anne's. She plotted and schemed quite shamelessly. "I'll try to persuade Mother Superior to buy Maribel a new dress, too."

"If you ask me, she needs new britches. I could only find one pair this morning. And she needs the ones with elastic in the legs." Emily Louise continued, "It's a mystery to me what happens to all her britches. They go to the laundry and that's the last we see of them."

Sister Mary Sophia said quietly, "I just brought over seven pair. I found them in the Sisters' laundry. Whoever sorted the linens down there must have thought . . ." She stopped, unable to mention what it was the linen sorters must have thought. "I should be back around noon."

Emily Louise made beds and washed backs. She attended to Mrs. Pleoski, who only wished to be left alone and not attended to at all. Then, while Bob was still busy with the men, she made her way to Room Two.

Miss Freidmann viewed the arrival of Emily Louise with a mixture of relief and alarm. The relief part disappeared entirely with the girl's first words. "See what I've got for you," Emily Louise was saying cheerfully. "A hair rinse. Want a hair-do today?"

"Hair rinse?" Miss Freidmann gasped. "Now see here, you're not dyeing my hair."

"Oh." For a moment Emily Louise was distracted as she surveyed a new pile of magazines on the stand. "Don't tell me Dickey Bird has been back again already?"

"If you mean Mr. Dickey, the lawyer, yes. He has been back. He came last night and brought the magazines." Miss Freidmann sighed. "I wish he had brought something smaller. I can't hold these in my hands."

"Then you'd better exercise your pinkies, Dearie. And don't let on to him that you can't hold a magazine. Maybe it's true that men like their women to be helpless, especially in bed. But, having crooked fingers is not being helpless in exactly the right kind of way, if you get what I mean. Men," Emily Louise went on candidly, "look out for themselves. They like a woman to act helpless as long as they are sure she's as strong as an ox underneath. Or unless she's rich, then they'll take her any old way."

"I'm not rich."

"I didn't suppose you were or you wouldn't be here at Saint Anne's. Pity, though. Just think, if you had lots of money you could lie in bed and have maids and servants at your beck and call. You could even be an invalid and still be glamorous. But seeing you are neither rich, and to be honest, not very glamorous either, we'll do the best we can with what you have. And we'll start right off with your hair. We'd better get it done before Dickey Bird comes too often, or else he will notice the change."

"You're not dyeing my hair. I don't care if I am gray. You'd think I was trying to catch the man."

"Well, aren't you? There's no use getting all coy about it. After all, lawyer or not, a man's a man. And with so many of them off to war, we can't be too particular. Besides," she continued, "Sister Mary Sophia is away this morning so this would be a good time to get it done. Not that she'd mind. I'm sure it's no worse then Mrs. Pleoski smoking her pipe."

"It's a fine state of affairs if the patients at Saint Anne's have to choose between smoking pipes and getting their hair dyed. You can take that little package and throw it right away."

"Oh no you don't, Dearie. I squandered twenty-nine cents on that hair rinse. Now we are going to use it."

"Throw it out. I'll give you twenty-nine cents."

"I wouldn't think of it. It will be worth the money to see you looking younger."

As Emily Louise bustled about, Miss Freidmann could only stare in dismay at the paraphernalia she accumulated. Miss Freidmann never had her hair washed any more than was absolutely necessary. It was a painful process that meant having pillow after pillow pushed low under her back until, finally, her head and neck just hung in space. She grimaced as, inch by inch, Emily Louise propped her higher and then clipped a brown rubber sheet around her neck. Miss Freidmann had never minded the rubber sheet part before. Now, after the confidences of Emily Louise, she found herself sniffing cautiously and wondering what had been its previous occupation.

Emily Louise fingered the hair. "It's too long. I'm going to cut it a bit. No use to wash any more than we have to."

"I don't want it cut. As soon as it grows a bit more I'm going to have it braided. It will be neater that way."

"Neater, that it will. I once knew a gardener who braided the tops of his onions while he waited for them to dry. They were neater, but they weren't much in the way of beauty.

And who wants a head like an onion? Let's clip it. It will freshen you up a bit."

As she spoke, Emily Louise tried an experimental clip. Critically, she held aloft the dismembered lock. "See what I mean, gray and coarse. Looks like a horse's mane."

Miss Freidmann's voice trembled her alarm, "Where did that come from?"

"Off the top of your head, Dearie. Where do think?"

"You can't cut a piece of hair like that, right off the top of my head. It will look silly."

"That's exactly what I mean. It does look silly. Now if you'll just hold still, I'll balance it up a bit."

The scissors clipped steadily and the gray strands, whole long lengths of them, fell and slid down the brown rubber sheet. Then, Emily Louise brought a bowl and started to pour the warm water through Miss Freidmann's hair.

The warmth was soothing. Miss Freidmann remembered that she hadn't had her hair washed since before Christmas. She said, "Something in that water smells funny. What is it?"

"Sometimes we get a patient in with lice. Stubborn wee beasties they are, too."

"For Goodness sake. I've been here for five years. You ought to know I haven't got lice."

"And I've been here less than one. But, there's one thing I've learned at Saint Anne's and that's to be prepared for anything."

"Ooohh, you've got water in my ear. What are you doing now?"

"Rinsing."

Miss Freidmann turned her eyes to the side and saw that the little envelope had disappeared from the stand. "You're not using that dye?"

"Rinse, Dearie. It sounds better. And sure, it's using it I am. Don't move now, or they'll be wondering at the laundry what color of sheets will be coming down next. Oh, but you're going to look beautiful."

"You're getting me all wet."

"That's because you're sliding down in the bed. Hoist yourself up a bit."

"I can't hoist myself up. You'll have to help me."

"If I do, you'll have a pan full of black dye in your bed. It won't only be your hair that's tinted."

"Oh," Miss Freidmann said irritably. "Why didn't you put the sandbag under my knees? That's the only thing that stops me from sliding."

"Well, I didn't. Your precious sandbag is on the stand. Your knees are virgin pure and on their own. If you slide down one more inch, you will tip this bowl full of water, and if I let go to help you, it will spill, too. You'd better ring the buzzer. Maybe Bob will come."

"Bob? My nightgown is all undone. Good Heavens, my chest is bare."

"And flat, too, Dearie. If you couldn't see the brown dots, you'd never know they were there. Ring for Bob and you'd better hurry or we'll have black dye from one end of you to the other."

"Won't it wash off?" Miss Freidmann panicked and her wildly fluttering hand closed about the buzzer.

"It says on the package, 'guaranteed not to streak or run.' You'd better push long and hard or Bob will never come." As they waited, Emily Louise confided, "This is the first time I ever tried washing a patient's hair in bed."

"Well, I wish you had done your practicing on someone else." Miss Freidmann tried to pull the nightgown up over her chest.

"You'd better get your fingers back on that buzzer. You're slipping further and the bowl is tipping more every minute."

"Where do you suppose he is?"

"Bob? Oh, he's either giving enemas or baths. It might take him a little while to get away."

Miss Freidmann gritted her teeth and pressed her bent finger with all her might against the little knob of the buzzer.

There was a light knock on the door. "Miss Emily, are you there?"

"Yes. In here, Bob. We need you. Come on in and," Emily Louise added as the burly form entered the room, "shut one eye, Bob. Her chest is bare and she's modest. You needn't worry," she reassured Miss Freidmann, "as long as he's got one eye shut. He'd need both eyes to see them."

Bob delicately pulled up the sheet. As he leaned over the bed, Miss Freidmann had a glimpse of a face, lined and creased by a smile, coming closer and closer to her own. She shut her eyes as she felt his hand slide under her shoulders and the other move beneath her legs until his bare forearm rested practically right up against her bottom. Momentarily, the pain of the movement was forgotten as she felt strong fingers press into her flesh and lift her, bodily, up in the bed. And she lay, waiting for the movement of his hands, firm and strong, as they slid out from under her again.

Never, Miss Freidmann realized with a rush, had a man's fingers brushed with such intimacy upon her anatomy. And never had she felt such a strange trembling to her body. She opened her eyes and knew, with some relief, that her emotions had gone unnoticed.

Bob's eyes were on Emily Louise who was carefully arching her body away from the basin, which was dripping it's black water down her hand. "Any time you need help, Miss Emily, call on me."

Miss Freidmann was aware from the look on his face that Bob knew all about Emily Louise. Knew all about her and liked her. There was open admiration in his blue eyes as they followed the movements of her body. "Any time you need me, Miss Emily," he repeated softly.

And while Miss Freidmann pondered the meaning of his words, the girl answered, "Thanks, Bob. I knew I could count on you."

Was this ordinary conversation, Miss Freidmann wondered? Or was it . . . it sounded like . . . some sort of promise. When Bob had gone, she lay and watched the rounded lines of Emily Louise's breasts as she bent over the bed. She looked at the smooth softness of the girl's body and envied her.

For the first time, Miss Freidmann had felt the firmness of a man's hand upon her flesh. Her buttocks still tingled where Bob's fingers had pressed into her body. Emily Louise had felt all these things. All these and many more. It might be good to have her hair dyed. Only Mr. Dickey wouldn't have very firm fingers. Miss Freidmann felt disappointment over the state of Mr. Dickey's fingers, even while her face reddened at the boldness of her reflections. However, her thoughts, as though freed by the touch of Bob's fingers, came crowding in and would not be denied.

She was young. Not yet thirty. And yet, all these things had passed her by. And had, in the passing, left her bent and ugly.

Always, when Emily Louise worked with her, she pushed the bed away from the wall and left it in line with the mirror. Miss Freidmann watched the girl now, rumpling and drying her hair with a towel, a towel which was quite rapidly becoming smudged with black. "Goodness, girl, the whole bed will be black. What will Sister Mary Sophia say?"

"Sister Mary Sophia won't say a word. I'll change the cases. Besides, the black's not supposed to rub off once it's dry. There now, aren't you beautiful?' Emily Louise had combed the hair up from Miss Freidmann's forehead and away from her face. "Lucky Mama bequeathed you her wavy hair. You look at least ten years younger."

"Do you think so?" Miss Freidmann gazed at her reflection in the mirror with a sudden buoyancy. "I think I do look a little better. But hardly nineteen again."

"I didn't say that, Dearie. I only said you looked ten years younger. You looked at least forty-five before. Now we've got you down to about thirty-five. We've still got plenty to accomplish and not much to accomplish it with, if I may say so."

"Thirty-five isn't so bad."

"An oldish thirty-five. But then, Rome wasn't built in a day and things go pretty slow at Saint Anne's. Even dying takes an age. There's Mrs. Pleoski, been going for weeks and even Fourteen."

"For Goodness sake, girl, can't you talk of something cheerful?"

"I try, my Pretty. But there's nothing much to be cheerful about, with everyone either mad or dying and some of them both at the same time."

"I'm not dying and I'm not mad."

"You are neither, bless you. Skinny as you are, you should hang on for a good few years yet. And old Dickey Bird will keep you sane. Now, don't you go telling him you've had your hair done and he'll never notice. Men are all as conceited as toads anyway. He'll think just seeing him has made you bloom with youth again. And remember," she added shrewdly, "you may look like Mama, but you are Papa's daughter, too. Keep him coming, but don't sign anything."

"He hasn't asked me to sign anything."

"He will. He's a sly one. A magpie Dickey bird, I'd say. You know, they sit on fence posts, preening their feathers, the picture of shining innocence. Then the minute your back's turned, whoosh, and they're off with a chicken. Not that you're much of a chicken, Dearie," Emily Louise patted Miss Friedmann's cheek, "but just watch out you don't get plucked."

For some time after Emily Louise had gone, Miss Freidmann continued to look at herself in the mirror. It was a stranger she saw there. Five years at Saint Anne's and the face in the mirror was that of a stranger. Still, whatever Emily Louise said, it wasn't such a bad face. There were finely curved eyebrows above the dark eyes. And there had been long lashes. She supposed they were still long, she was too far from the mirror to tell. A long time ago, she had used a lipstick and she pressed her lips together, making the color come back to them. Still, the face disappointed her.

Miss Freidmann gazed critically at her reflected features. It was a down face. That was it. The lines about her eyes drooped down. Her mouth sagged. That was the only word for it, sagged. She looked away and clutched at the magazine, dragging it awkwardly from the stand. Slowly, her fingers turned the pages. Too slowly. The pictures all had a sameness. Battle scenes, tanks, guns, and now in February of 1945, of returning soldiers. Wounded and crippled, many of them. Hailed as heroes. A soldier could lose an arm or a leg and count on sympathy. Miss Freidmann could count on nothing except the suddenly dismal sameness of the routine at Saint Anne's. And Sunday, when Mr. Dickey had hinted he might come again, stretched through the sameness, four long days away.

Miss Freidmann allowed the magazine to fall heavily against her knees. From across the hall, above the sound of running water and clattering metal, came the warbling voice of Emily Louise, "If you know any ladies, who want any babies, just send them along to me . . ."

The girl was shameless. Absolutely shameless. But she had lived. And while she reflected on Emily Louise and her living, the pain crept back into Miss Freidmann's limbs. It throbbed from her toes to her knees, to her shoulders and wrists, until her body was torn and there was no thought in her mind but the misery of it. Carefully, she edged her freshly exposed neck into the shelter of the pillow and the newly darkened hair tumbled over the white linen. But, the old lines pulled her lips down and fell about her eyes when, at last, she slept.

CHAPTER 5

It was Sunday afternoon and Miss Freidmann, propped high in her bed, sat and stared at her visitor in dismay. Exactly as Emily Louise had predicted, Mr. Dickey came bearing a bouquet of roses.

How had that girl known he would bring roses? Miss Freidmann could hear her now, 'When he brings flowers, they'll be roses. He's that type.' The entire effect was ruined.

She watched, fascinated, as he went over and lay the flowers on the dresser and the blossoms spilled, with scarlet defiance, from the confining green of the paper. Then, she averted her eyes and managed a careful, "How very kind."

Mr. Dickey sensed no disappointment, apparently. "I always liked flowers in a sick room," he said. "Cheerful, don't you think? How are you feeling today?" He looked at her and his eyes widened. "I must say, you look better. Much better. The change is absolutely amazing." He picked up one of her twisted hands, looked at it and put it back down again on the white spread. Turning, he pulled up a chair.

Miss Freidmann lay with her eyes fixed on her own hand. Again, she felt the disappointment and it threatened at any moment to give way to downright irritation. There were other ways of holding a woman's hand. Bob's way, for instance. Bob's fingers hadn't been gripping her hand. She said, looking at his reddened ears, "Is it cold outside?"

"A little," he answered. "I hurried. I didn't want the flowers to get frozen."

The roses were demanding attention again. She said, a little sharply, "You could have put some extra paper over them."

"So I could. Men are thoughtless about things like

that."

"Are they?" Miss Freidmann tried to think of something to say. Anything, just to get away from the flowers. What was there to talk about when one had lived at Saint Anne's and had only known and spoken of pain, one's own pain, for five years?

Mr. Dickey ventured into the silence. "As your lawyer," he said and hesitated, "there's, ah . . . a little business matter I should discuss with you."

"Yes?" So it was going to be business and Emily Louise would be right again.

"It's about your house."

"What about my house?"

"Well, you know it's been rented ever since," again he hesitated, "ever since you came here."

"It's been rented for five years," she stated flatly, annoyed at his hesitation. From the way he hemmed and hawed, she might have been in jail. "As a matter of fact, it's been more than five years. Nearly five and a half."

"Yes, indeed," he agreed. "For over five years. And now, it's come to my attention, actually the tenants brought it to my attention, there's been no repairs on the place in all those years. The house needs . . ." he took a breath, ". . . the house needs repair and it needs redecorating."

"Redecorating?"

"Painting and so on."

"Then it will have to be painted. Get it done and take the money out of the rent."

He walked over to the window and stood looking down on the street below. His shoulders, she noticed, weren't broad like Bob's. They seemed drooped and narrow. "Unfortunately," he continued without looking at her, "there's going to be more than paint. There's the roof, it's old and leaky. And the heating system. Absolutely insufficient. I understand it's too cold for the baby."

"You mean those renters have a baby? In Mama's parlor?"

"Well, they have a baby. I suppose it's in the parlor. And

that's another thing, one of the legs is broken off the dining table."

"At least I should think they could repair their own table."

"Miss Freidmann, it isn't their table. It's yours."

"Mine?"

"Of course. The house was rented fully furnished."

"You don't mean to tell me Mama's lovely furniture is still in that house with renters and a baby. Get it out of there at once. Mama's lovely furniture." Miss Freidmann closed her eyes as she remembered, for the first time in many years, the soft pastels and the polished oak in Mama's parlor. "Let them buy their own table."

Mr. Dickey spoke with a hint of impatience, "Surely you knew the house was rented furnished, after all this time?"

"Mr. Dickey," Miss Freidmann's voice was sharpened by the vision of a table with a broken leg. Why, it was a solid oak table and it would have taken a baby elephant to break one of those legs. "Mr. Dickey," she repeated, "when I came in here, I was ill. Very ill, do you understand? I don't remember making any arrangements about renters or furniture or anything else. I always assumed Ames & Bates would have the sense to look after things. I was in too much pain to think about houses or furniture." The mention of her pain, unpredictably, took the defiance from her voice. "I'm still ill," she whimpered. "I'm still in pain."

"Yes, of course, you are," He picked up her hand and looked uncomfortable as his eyes rested upon the bent deformity of her fingers. He patted them, awkwardly. "You just tell me what you want to do and I'll take care of everything."

The sympathy brought back her courage. "I want Mama's furniture taken out of that house."

"My dear Miss Freidmann," he said patiently. "If you take out that furniture, you won't get so much rent."

"I don't care. Take it out."

"What shall I do with it?"

"Have it crated and stored in the basement."

"The basement," he hesitated, "I believe the basement is being used."

"Whatever for?"

"I'm not sure. But there is the furnace and the coal room and I suppose the room is taken up. In any event," he said with finality, "you won't be able to store the furniture in there."

"You get that furniture out of that house."

"All right, if you insist, but you won't get so much rent. And, really, now that the table is ruined and they've been using it for five years, you might just as well leave it there."

He was right, of course. If they'd managed to break that table, the rest of the furnishings were probably ruined.

Mr. Dickey seemed to sense his advantage. He continued, quickly, "You might as well keep the rent up as high as you can. You are going to have to put in a new furnace and probably a new roof."

"What's wrong with the roof?"

"It leaks."

"Can't it be patched or something?"

"It's leaked upstairs and the plaster has all come down. Miss Freidmann," he made a determined effort, "it is going to cost you at least a thousand dollars to fix up that house."

"A thousand dollars?" Miss Freidmann jerked her head and it hurt. Dollars were made for comfort. Bodily comfort. Not for houses. Why, for an opened dollar box of candy on her dresser, the girls in blue would adjust the heat and pull down the shades for weeks.

Miss Freidmann had a lot of respect for a dollar and infinitely more respect for Papa, who had left her with a supply of them. And Papa had not accumulated his dollars by scattering them willy-nilly on leaking roofs and smoky furnaces. If only she was more like Mama. Mama would have just leaned back and waved her hand and said, "All right, have it repaired. Simon will take care of the bill."

Miss Freidmann suddenly knew, black hair or not, she wasn't in the least like Mama. And anyway, Simon Freidmann wasn't there to take care of the bill. She acknowledged her Papa's caution. A thousand dollars, indeed. Why, the man was crazy. A repeated twinge in the bones of her neck only increased her irritation. "Papa," she said, "used to have a man come in on Saturdays to do odd jobs and repairs. I think he paid him five dollars a day."

Mr. Dickey was condescending, but polite. "Times have changed, Miss Freidmann. The war, you know. You can't find a man to work on Saturday or any other day for five dollars. You've been here too long. You're out of touch."

Out of touch, was she? Well, she would just tell Mr. Dickey. Only she didn't tell Mr. Dickey.

The roses glowed with the red of velvet over on the dresser. The pains were sharper in her neck and reaching out for her shoulders. She was out of touch. He was right. And he was in touch. Furthermore, he was a man. After five years and an endless parade of women in white and girls in blue, there was a man who had come to call and talk with her. "I'm tired," she whimpered. "There is a little handle at the end of the bed. Could you roll me down?"

"Of course," he said and his voice was assured and soothing. "How selfish of me. I've talked too long and tired you. You just think it all over and we'll discuss it later on."

"Later on," she grasped at the words.

"I'll come back, later on." He took her hand in his. "It may be a week or so, but I'll be back."

A thousand dollars, it was utterly ridiculous. His hand, in the gesture of a hand shake, rested lightly around her fingers. Still, if he had to have the money to repair the house, then he would have to have it. She was about to tell him so when her eyes again encountered the roses and the velvet red was only a warning that spoke with the voice of Emily Louise, "Remember, you're Papa's daughter. Don't sign anything."

Miss Freidmann stirred her hand slightly and it was

Mama Freidmann's daughter who lay feeling the sensuous warmness of a man's touch course from her fingers through her warped and twisted body. However, it was Simon Freidmann's daughter who, with pain brightening her eyes, gazed at the man by her bed, thrilled to the strangeness of his touch and said calmly, "Yes, that will be much better. We will discuss it later on."

He left and she decided to sleep. Sleep quickly, so she would have the strength to face Emily Louise. But, let the girl laugh and tease, she wouldn't care. Miss Freidmann pushed away thoughts of the thousand dollars and concentrated on Mr. Dickey. He was a man. He had called on her, Theresa Freidmann, bent, crippled, bedridden, and twenty-nine years old. He had brought her flowers and she was sure . . . it really seemed that his touch had been lingering as he bade her farewell. The sleep Miss Freidmann slept was one of satisfaction.

A voice, mocking as the red hair mocked the roses, awakened her. "Having gay and naughty dreams, I'll wager."

"Go away and let me sleep."

"Hmmm, an even dozen. I'll bet he got a rate. Didn't I tell you he'd bring roses?"

"How did you know?" Miss Freidmann opened her eyes and knew she shouldn't have asked.

"He's just that type. You know, no imagination. Carnations for weddings and funerals and roses for everything else. Pity, isn't it? Just think what you could feel for a man who was bold enough to bring you a yellow daffodil in the middle of a Saskatchewan winter. A man who is bold with flowers could be bold with other things, too."

"What sort of things?"

"Now, now, Dearie. Sometimes I think you aren't as sick as you pretend to be. I'll tell you, though, a man can be bold about any amount of things. But not your Dickey Bird. He's not the type. Hidebound, I'd say. But don't let it bother you." Emily Louise was cheerful. "Most men are. Reminds me of the time my daddy won the championship with his Angus bull and he brought Mother some flowers. Do you know what he brought her, and she as Irish as Kilarney? A bowl of Scotch heather. He did bring her a new silk nightgown, though, emerald green as though she'd picked it out herself. Only four sizes too small. Mother just kept it under her pillow and wore her old flannelette. She said if he hadn't used his imagination with the heather, he was going to have to use it with that nightgown."

Miss Freidmann became lost, as usual, in the chattering of Emily Louise. "I don't," she said, "see any reason for keeping a nightgown four sizes too small under one's pillow."

"It isn't an earthly reason, Dearie. It's more apt to be a heavenly one. But take it from me, under the pillow is the very best place to leave a silk nightgown. And, speaking of nightgowns, you ought to have a few yourself. Do wonders to perk you up, you know, a bit of lace and a frill. Might even perk up old Dickey Bird as well."

"I don't see why I should buy nightgowns. There are plenty here."

"Sure. And who wears them? The old boys in room Eight and Mrs. Pleoski. Even Fourteen. I'd buy you a couple myself, if I didn't have the bill."

"Do you mean to tell me," Miss Freidmann spoke carefully, "that those old men wear the same nightgowns that I do?"

"That they do, my girl. And why not? A shimmy is a shimmy. Anyway, you are all the same from the bottom up."

Miss Freidmann eyed her stiff, white gown with distaste and made a rapid decision. "When you have your next day off, I'll give you the money and you can buy me one or two. I have no idea what they cost."

"You're out of touch."

"That's exactly what Mr. Dickey just told me."

"He did, did he? Well, you can be sure that he isn't. What you need is the paper. There's one down at the end of the hall. I'll bring it in and you can look over the ads. If you see something that catches your fancy, let me know and I'll pick it up for you the next time I'm in town."

The advertisements Emily Louise had recommended did not catch Miss Freidmann's fancy. They did, however, catch her eye. She couldn't remember just when she had last looked at a newspaper, but an entire era must have passed by. Or had she been insulated by the night shirts, the swathed sheets, and the nun's habits at Saint Anne's? Vaguely, she groped with her memories and gamely she tried to cope with the transformation. If Canada's men were at war, it looked as though her women were determined to give them something to come home to. Breasts bulged with patriotic pride beneath the flying Union Jacks that proclaimed the war time specials. And if bottoms were bringing up the rear, it was purely a structural limitation.

Miss Freidmann's fingers, curling into the pages of the newspaper, quivered and trembled. And when Emily Louise came back into the room, she said in a burst of rashness, "There is a ten dollar bill in my purse. You can take it and get me a nightgown. Any kind of nightgown, just so I don't have to wear the same ones as those old men. And tell Sister Mary Sophia I need a pill. I can't bear the pain in my knees another moment."

There was an unaccustomed gentleness in Emily Louise's reply. "Poor Dear. It's been a rough day. Roses and nightgowns and old Dickey Bird. Just wait until he sees you when we get through. He will warble like a meadowlark. I'll tell Sister Mary Sophia right way about the pill."

Miss Freidmann, in the days that followed, developed a simple cold. Her firm conviction that the cold was directly attributable to the hair rinsing did not allay her suffering in the least. She surrendered her body to the vicious barbs that tore at her joints and sought the mercy of the little white pills. And the pills only took her to a nightmare world where dollar bills blew from her clutching fingers to vanish in a thorny forest of broken table legs and scarlet roses.

She was recalled from the forest by Emily Louise. "Wake up, Dearie. I have a surprise for you."

Miss Freidmann kept her eyes closed as the words sank into her consciousness. Emily Louise was enough. The surprise would be more than she could bear. Regardless of the thorns and the vanishing dollars, she made her decision for the forest. Sighing, she turned her face to the wall. "Go away. My knees hurt. I want to rest."

"Hold still while I jiggle your sandbag and your knees will feel better in a jiffy. Probably been in one position too long. Come on, up we go, now. Look here, what I've got for you."

Miss Freidmann would have objected to the speed with which Emily Louise was raising her bed had her attention not been taken by the bold and garish garments overflowing from a brown paper sack and spreading across the bed. "What on Earth have you got there?"

"These, Dearie, are your nightgowns. A come-hither yellow and a pinch-me pink. Aren't they glamorous?"

"They just look cold to me. Why didn't you get something warm?"

"Summer's coming on. Besides, these will show you off better."

"There's no doubt about them showing me off. You can see right through them."

"I know, Dearie. I thought of that. I would have got you a nice little bed jacket, but I didn't have enough money. I did get this though. I thought as long as we were seeing through, we might as well have something there to see."

"What in the world is that?"

"A brassiere."

Miss Freidmann said irritably, "I know it's a brassiere. What's in it? What makes it stick out like that?"

"Falsies."

"Falsies? What do you think I'm going to do with . . . with falsies?"

"Wear them. Or maybe let them wear you. Tricky, aren't

they? Just like nature's own. Now, when you get dressed in the morning, you will be able to look down and see yourself all blossomed out. It'll do wonders for you. Every woman needs a chest." Emily Louise untied the tapes of Miss Freidmann's nightshirt. "Come on, let's try it on. I only got a thirty-two. You're that thin. I didn't think you ought to come in to full bloom too quickly."

The goose pimples raised on Miss Freidmann's arms as Emily Louise tossed aside the night shirt. "I've been ill," she said. "I daren't catch another cold."

"I know, Dearie, and I've got the heat turned up high." With cool, firm fingers, Emily Louise fastened the brassiere and ran her hands experimentally under the padded breasts. "Ummm," she nodded, approvingly. "Lifts you up, just right. Now the nightgown. Shall we have the pink or the yellow?"

"I don't care. Just get something over me and cover me up."

"Quick as a wink, Dearie." Emily Louise worked with a flurry of color and softness. "Did I tell you, I looked up your precious lawyer the other day? Not too prosperous, if you ask me. The office is over a hardware. But, I guess he's on the up and up. His name is on the door all nice and legal like."

"I expected it would be and I don't know why you should take the trouble to look."

"Oh, I just wanted to look out for you, and besides, my daddy told me never to go trusting lawyers."

Miss Freidmann was cold and miserable. She said, sharply, "I don't think you always listened so carefully to what your daddy said."

"You think not?" Emily Louise was unabashed. "Well, he never discussed anything like that with me. He just made sure Jamie went to court his girl on horseback and he left the worry of me to Mother." Emily Louise went on, lightly, "You know, I did ask Mother once all about babies and where they came from. She told me the doctor brought them in his little black bag. I asked her how he knew which one to leave where and she said he matched them up by the color of their hair. That seemed reasonable enough, too, because when I looked at Jamie's baby picture, sure enough, he was just like Daddy with no hair at all." Emily Louise shook her own bright head. "I was always a bit worried about myself, though, because I never knew another soul for miles around with red hair. I just thought the poor doctor had me left on his hands and he had to take a chance and leave me somewhere. And Mother being a one, with a kitchen full of stray cats and all, he figured she would be a good bet. Dear Mother," Emily Louise stepped back to gaze at the pink nightgown she had slipped over Miss Freidmann's head, "aren't you a pleasure to behold, though? Just wait until old Dickey sees you now."

"I don't know why you want to dress me up in pink nightgowns for Mr. Dickey's benefit. You've just been telling me I shouldn't trust him."

"I know. I'm just an old softie when it comes to romance. No use to worry about the worm when you're eating the apple. Just go ahead and enjoy it. Chances are, you won't find the worm until you get to the core and by that time, you've had all you want anyway. Besides," she finished, brightly, "perhaps he will fall so madly in love, he will forget all his wicked intentions."

Miss Freidmann chose to ignore Mr. Dickey's intentions. She said, "My arms are cold. I'll freeze in this thing. You will have to get more on me than this."

"So I shall, Dearie. And I still wish I had got you that little bed jacket I saw. Did I tell you about it? All soft and cuddly, it was, with a bit of fluff about the neck and sleeves. It was, you might say, a bit suggestive, but it was four ninety-eight and I'd spent every bit of your money."

"Do you mean to tell me you spent that whole ten dollars on . . . on these?"

"That I did. And I had to do some dime store shopping to manage it, too. I saved on the brassiere. I figured you didn't need an expensive one, there not being much of a weight there to hold up. I've got my daddy's eye for a bargain, so I have, and I should think you'd be grateful."

"Well, I'm not. Ten dollars usually lasts me a month. I don't own a mint, you know. Besides," and the urge to confide banished all her discretion, "Mr. Dickey says it is going to take a thousand dollars to fix up my house."

"He isn't wasting much time. Don't you think a thousand dollars is a bit steep for the first touch?"

Miss Freidmann was defensive, "He's probably right. The house hasn't had a dollar spent on it in five years. He says it needs a new roof and a new furnace and some paint. What annoyed me most," and Emily Louise noted with surprise that Miss Freidmann actually was annoyed, "he said the house had been rented furnished all these years. Furnished, mind you, with all of Mama's lovely furniture. I suppose it's all ruined by now. I'd just like to see it."

"Didn't you know it was rented furnished?"

Miss Freidmann answered sharply, "No, I didn't know it was rented furnished. Mr. Dickey asked me the same thing. Can't any of you understand what it's like to be ill?"

"There, there, Dearie. I guess we've never had rheumatics, if that's what you mean. And you seem to know what's going on about you now."

"Well, I didn't then. My arthritis started after Mama died. Every bone and joint in my body seemed to start swelling at once. And when Papa died, I couldn't even go to his funeral. They took me down town to the hospital and began giving me pills. I don't remember making any arrangements about anything . . ." In her dejection, Miss Freidmann allowed her head to sag and at once, she found her vision dominated by her chest. A chest which rose to unbelievable heights and obviously had not the slightest inclination to sag. She looked up quickly, "I don't know where he thinks I'm going to get a thousand dollars."

"Where did you get the ten you gave me?"

"Ames & Bates sent it to me. They collect the rent and pay Saint Anne's. In fact, they advised I be moved over here. Saint Anne's is cheaper and my rent money, along with the interest from Papa's bank account, pays my expenses and gives me a little spending money. That way, I don't have to use the principal. Papa left a comfortable bank account, but Ames & Bates takes care of all the statements. I'm not sure, exactly, how much there is."

"Well, I'll bet old Dickey Bird knows. And you can be sure there is a thousand dollars or he wouldn't be asking for it."

"Oh, there's more than a thousand there. A good deal more. I'm sure of that, but I have to be careful. I have no way of making any more. And suppose I had to go back to a regular hospital? You know, they are expensive."

"That they are, Dearie, so don't go handing your pennies over to visiting lawyers. Besides, how can you be sure the house needs all those repairs?"

"I don't know. I suppose I'll have to take his word for it."

"Get someone to look at it for you," Emily Louise said practically.

Miss Freidmann's voice was suddenly despairing, "I have no one. Friends seem to forget after five years."

"That's the trouble, you see. Now if you just had a religion you'd have a minister or a priest. And he would never forget you. At least, not so long as you had a house and a bank account and no one to leave it to when you're gone."

"I'm tired and I'm cold," Miss Freidmann said, wearily. "I'd like to forget the whole affair. And my arms will ache all night if you don't get me something besides this . . . this cobweb."

"I'll go and ask Sister Mary Sophia. I think she has a sweater tucked away in the linen closet." Emily Louise turned at the door. "And if that is a cobweb, then it was spun by a passionate spider. You look downright ravishing. Just keep old Dickey flying for another week and I'll go and look at the house for you, myself."

Miss Freidmann hunched her shoulders and impatiently waited for Emily Louise to return with the sweater.

She didn't know just what to make of the girl. First, there had been the hair rinse and now she was all decked out with this bosom. Those things were absolutely indecent and she couldn't get her hands behind her back to get them off. Perhaps the sweater would hide them. On the other hand, there was a soft comfort to the nightgown, a clinging about her body that somehow seemed to soothe. She leaned back carefully, unwilling, in spite of herself, to crease the newness of the gown. It was nice of Emily Louise to offer to look at the house. When she had more money, she would let the girl go and buy a bed jacket, a warm one, seeing she enjoyed making such purchases.

And she must remember to ask for a pill. One never knew when the pain would come again. There was only the certainty that it would come.

Emily Louise didn't find a sweater. She came with the blue-striped top of a pair of man's pajamas and she slipped it about Miss Freidmann's shoulders.

"Whose is that? Where did that come from?" Miss Freidmann's voice was shrill.

"Goodness knows, Dearie. It's been on the shelf for months. The owner has probably long since passed on. Never mind. It will keep your arms cozy and it's a contrast to the pink. Sister Mary Sophia was happy to find a use for it. She hates to see anything go to waste."

"If it's some old man's . . ."

"Now don't get alarmed, my Pretty. What's wrong with a man's pajamas in your bed? Better than a sandbag. They'll add flavor to your dreams."

They were dreams Miss Freidmann had to conjure for herself. Long after Emily Louise had gone, she remembered that she'd forgotten again to ask for the pill.

CHAPTER 6

It was a Sunday afternoon in early March that Emily Louise chose to appraise the condition of Miss Freidmann's house.

Emily Louise had slept late, arising just in time to attend the eleven o'clock Mass. She lingered to eat lunch at Saint Anne's, which was always of roast beef on Sundays, and anyway, her bill rather excluded the possibility of eating downtown. Now, standing before her mirror, she deliberately selected a black bandanna and tied it about her head. She wore it, not to subdue herself, but only to subdue the rebellious glow of her hair. Then, she stepped with delight into the March day.

She stepped with equal delight into her memories. One deep breath of the air with its promise of spring and it was no longer March of 1945. It was March a year ago.

She boarded the street car and slid far to the inside of the seat, so "he" could come and sit beside her. A smile touched her lips as she pictured him, tall, swaying with the motion of the coach, walking down the aisle toward her. She almost felt the roughness of his Air Force great coat nudging her shoulder. And she saw him, head bent, officers cap pushed back, one black curl drooping down toward his eyebrow. She even heard him say, "That's how it goes, my Love. Uncle George says, 'We must have the boys of Number Three Squad. And you, Flying Officer O'Shaughnessy, must stay until they are graduated.' No romance in his heart at all, that Uncle George. And never let it be said that His Majesty's Royal Canadian Air Force would let Old England down. So my furlough's been delayed for seven more days." And she could feel his tenderness again, "Is it so bad, my Sweetheart, that we must wait for one more week? We'll be married right after the graduation and have my two week furlough for a honeymoon."

Emily Louise clung to her reverie and watched as Saskatoon passed the street-car window. There were all the streets she knew so well. There was the cafe where she had worked. The cafe where she had first glimpsed Irish O'Shaughnessy. Where her heart had melted as quickly as the extra sugar lumps she had slipped him for his coffee. And down the street was the apartment building where she had stayed. And where he had stayed. For in truth, Old England notwithstanding, one more week had been too long to wait. And again, she felt the joy of him, the moment of lingering that had only meant surrender. Dear Mother, the surrender. She thrilled to the memory of the glorious love-filled nights of it. And she let her pounding heart drain itself anew, as it had that night when he didn't come, the night when she learned that Irish O'Shaughnessy had flown on and on and away.

She tugged at the black bandanna. Still, her thoughts took none of the somberness of the cloth. Rather, her spirit soared like his, free and happy in the soaring. She remembered, close in his arms in the darkness, she asked him, "Must you? Must you fly?"

And his answer, "My Sweet, it's a dream world up there. All the hustle and bustle is left behind and a man is all alone with all the sky to dream in." And so it was. If she must live her life with just a dream, and that dream was Irish O'Shaughnessy, then it had been worth it.

A girl with a baby boarded the street car and took his place beside her. Reluctantly, she let him go and turned her eyes to the child, noticing the wisp of black hair that pushed in front of the bonnet and the tiny fist folded about the blanket. "It's a wee boy," she said, impulsively.

The mother turned, smiling "How did you know? So many people think he looks like a girl. I'm glad someone knows."

"How old is he?" Emily Louise asked and spoke the words slowly so there would be no tremble in her voice.

"Three months, next week."

Her own would have been that age. Somewhere there

must be someone holding her son in a blue blanket, somewhere her son would have fingers curled in a tiny fist. "What is the baby's name?" She asked the question softly. "Joseph, Little Joe. His daddy is overseas. He hasn't seen the baby yet. He's going to be so proud. We both wanted a little boy," the girl confided.

Emily Louise watched the girl cradling the child in her arms. He hadn't been adopted, then. This was not to be some chance discovery of her own. Emily Louise knew a sudden, violent longing. And for the first time, she realized the life, and not the death, had been the real price of her dream.

The streetcar was quite empty by the time Emily Louise got off at Waverly Avenue. Miss Freidmann's house was certainly far enough from town, practically at the end of the car line. A glance at the house numbers and she knew she was going to have a long walk. Eight blocks. Emily Louise looked down at the high heels of her black pumps with dismay. The sidewalks had been free of snow at Saint Anne's and she had scorned the comfort of her old brown oxfords and the velvet overshoes. Still, there was no alternative, she would have to walk. At least the day was clear and sunny.

Emily Louise lifted her face to the blue sky and the wind. A few more weeks and the stubble fields would be bared on the farm. Spring wasn't the same in the city. Nothing to uncover except the grass squares between the paths and the sidewalks. Below her, the Saskatchewan River curled in its banks, waiting out the winter. It would sparkle again very soon and its edges would stretch in velvet ribbons across the prairie. Waverly Avenue must be one of the more select streets of Saskatoon. Trust Papa Freidmann to ensconce the members of his house in style.

Emily Louise was beginning to develop firm respect for Papa Freidmann. He had been a little like her own father, shrewd and confident. Men should be so. And their women, dependent and yielding. She grimaced a little at the thought. Irish O'Shaughnessy hadn't been particularly shrewd. He'd give his last nickel to a blind seller of shoelaces. However, he had been confident enough. Come to think of it, she wasn't exactly dependent, although, and when her eyes crinkled it wasn't against the wintery sun, no one could say she hadn't been yielding.

She still had three more blocks to go and the sidewalk had faded to a twisting path that crept forward from telephone pole to telephone pole. Native poplars clustered about the houses and screened them from the road. If she went much further, she would end up on the open prairie. Emily Louise quickened her pace to match her quickening curiosity.

She came upon the house and it did not surprise her. She knew it would be the one she sought, even before she read the number on the gate. Again, Papa Freidmann had not proved disappointing. The house was large. Rough, gray stone made it staunch and solid, and wooden pillars and porticos gave it an ageless grace and charm. Emily Louise walked slowly, her eyes searching for details. Old Dickey, she admitted with some reluctance, had been no more than right. The house was lovely, but it certainly needed the repairs. The wood was unpainted and weathered. Bricks had tumbled from the chimney and one front window was covered with a cardboard patch. Tall evergreens had been planted around the edge of the property. And again, Simon Freidmann had been generous. This was not a city lot. There was an acre or two of land here, and every bit of it covered with litter and trash. There was shrubbery that had spread with untrimmed abandon and a birdbath, white and symmetrical, where the amber edges of a broken beer bottle glinted in the sun. Three garbage cans were lined up by the gate and a cat, amber like the bottle, curled up on the only one that had a lid.

Watching the house, Emily Louise missed the twisting path. Momentarily, she lost her balance and then she grimaced as she felt the telltale wobble of her right shoe. She had loosened the heel of her only pair of dress shoes. She'd owe Saint Anne's forever. And then her face brightened. What better excuse than a broken shoe? She turned in the gate, passed the cat and the garbage cans, and limped her way down the path to the front door.

A girl's face appeared at the window on one side of the cardboard patch. Emily Louise encountered the child's eyes and knew she watched her all the way to the house, still watched her as she raised the brass knocker and let it fall against the heavy oak door. It was, she noticed, a solid door. Solid, as the house was solid, and like the house, scarred either by abuse or neglect. As she waited, a man's voice, rough and loud, spoke clearly from behind it.

"Mary Ann, go see who's at the door. And if it's some Sunday school teacher with a pile of scriptures, we don't want none."

The door opened and Emily Louise again found herself facing the girl from the window. She was a child of about ten, Emily Louise judged, blonde and wide-eyed. "Hello," she said, boldly, and somehow the word became a question.

"Hello." Emily Louise lifted her damaged shoe. "I've broken the heel off my shoe. I was wondering if you'd have a hammer?"

The man's voice broke in, "Mary Ann, for God's sake shut the door. Want we should heat up the whole outside?"

"Someone wants a shoe fixed."

"Well, we ain't the bloody shoemakers."

"It's," the girl hesitated, "a lady. Heel's broke off her shoe. You got a hammer?"

The voice growled, "Okay, then. Let her in. I used to be able to shoe a horse. Reckon I can pound the heel on a lady's slipper."

As Emily Louise entered the front room, the man rose somewhat unsteadily from a sagging overstuffed chair. A gin bottle on the chair arm swayed dangerously and he rescued it with concern. He looked then, in the general direction of the broken shoe, back to the gin bottle, and at last his glance encountered that of Emily Louise. "Want a drink?" he offered. "Ain't worth a damn, but it's about all you can get."

Emily Louise smiled and shook her head. He shrugged and the white undershirt stretched tighter over his hairy chest and shoulders. He poured some of the liquor into a glass and turned to splash it with a soft drink that stood open on the piano. His back, Emily Louise noticed, was nearly as hairy as his chest and the khaki army pants that didn't quite clear the crest of his stomach hung only by the grace of frayed suspenders. "Mary Ann," he said to the child who stood watching, "go and look down in the basement for a hammer. Damn street out there is just a rut," he volunteered. "Well, why shouldn't it be? It ain't going no place. Just to hell and gone. What you doing, walking down here, anyway?"

"To be truthful," Emily Louise said, deciding on honesty, "I was coming here. You see, I know your landlady and she was wondering about her house. She's in the hospital and she hasn't seen the place in five years."

"She ain't fixed it in that long, either," the man said abruptly, "but she ain't shy in taking the money. And if you know her, you can tell her I said so. Sure you won't have a drink?"

"No thank you," Emily Louise said and then confided, "You know, I never really cared much for gin."

"Can't blame you. Tastes like . . . Well, I reckon you're a lady so I ain't gonna tell you what it tastes like. But, what the hell. I can't get nothin' else on my permit and Annie wouldn't go get any yesterday."

From the stairs, there came an odd scream. "Jeez, there she goes again." He looked at the clock. "Right on the dot, every ten minutes." He sank morosely back into the chair. "A man gets home from the army twice every year, once at Christmas and once for a furlough. And what happens? Christmas, and all her kids get the measles. My furlough, and she's gotta have a baby. She's got three up there now and where she's going to put this one, God only knows. I'm glad I'm going back to Chilliwac next week."

Vividly, Emily Louise pictured Miss Freidmann's reaction to the renters in her house who were regularly producing babies. As she pondered, a woman with blonde hair like the child's came hurrying down the stairs. She glanced briefly at Emily Louise and said, urgently, "Pete, I think she's going to have it."

"Aw, Annie," he answered wearily. "You know how she is. Every time she gets a bellyache, she's going to have it. She's been gonna have it every day for the last week."

"Pete, you listen to me. I know she's going to have it. Call a cab."

"She got the money to pay for it? Her kids is always costing me money."

"Pete." A dark-haired girl leaned against the door, her voice high pitched and hysterical, her hand gripped her stomach. "I'm going to have it, Pete. Call a cab."

Together Emily Louise and Annie helped the girl to a chair. "Sit down, Dorothy, and try and be still," Annie soothed. "Pete will call a taxi."

"Oh, if only Lester was here," Dorothy wailed. "Les-ter, Les-ter. Help me, Les-ter."

"Kee-rist." Pete picked up the telephone and dialed a number that was scribbled, conveniently, on the wall. "Got a cab?" he asked. "Listen, the dame's havin' a kid. We need one in a hurry, and say," he wheedled, "have you got any liquor? Oh, hell, anything. I ain't proud. Anything at all and you better hurry. Women," he said and hung up the receiver, his eyes travelling from Annie to the huddled form of Dorothy. "Women and kids. You come home on furlough and the place is full of them. Can't get a hold on your own wife for some woman having kids. What you doin' now?" he asked plaintively, as Annie began to tie a white scarf over her head.

"Pete, I'll have to go with Dorothy," Annie said. "After all, she is my sister and she needs someone to go with her." She winked knowingly at Emily Louise. "You'll have to excuse my husband, sometimes he gets a little anxious."

"Well, Jeez, woman. What kind of furlough is it for a soldier when his wife spends all Saturday night cooped up with some woman having a baby?" And then, persuasively, "C'mon, Annie. Stay with me and have a drink."

"Oh, you big ape," she rumpled his hair. "I'll sleep with you tonight. I've got to take care of Dorothy as long as Lester is away."

"Les-ter," Dorothy broke down completely. "Lester," she cried. "My Lester. He's going overseas and he'll be killed and he'll never see the baby."

Pete emptied the bottle of gin into his glass, shook it for the last drop. "Hell, he's seen the other three, ain't he? Anyway, he won't get overseas. The war'll be over before he even sees the other side. And when this war is over, I'm gettin' the hell out of here." He suddenly remembered Emily Louise. "You can tell the landlady that, too. I'm going up north and I'm gonna set right in the middle of it and watch it grow. And there ain't gonna be no woman around having kids. Just the wind blowing and the wheat growing and not a woman around having a kid. Not even a cow having a calf."

"You taking me, Pete?" Annie asked.

"Goddamn right, I'm taking you, Annie. You and Mary Ann. And Mary Ann is all there's gonna be. A man's got to learn something in the army."

Pete stared about the room until his gaze rested on Dorothy. She sat, bent forward on the edge of the chair, her open coat revealing the expectant bulge of her stomach. "And Dorothy and Lester," he continued, "can just stack up here. Dorothy and Lester and all the rest like them. Crazy fools. Join the army and figure they got to get married and have kids before they die. Well, they can stack up here three deep with all their kids. They can live in their moldy old rented rooms and cook in community kitchens. I'm going out on the prairie." He emptied his glass. "And I'm gonna sit and drink rye whiskey. They can put this stuff back in the horse barn where it belongs."

"If Lester will only come back," Dorothy sobbed, "I'll live

with him anywhere."

"Of course, Lester will come back," Annie comforted. "He hasn't even left Montreal yet. And you heard what Pete said. The war will soon be over. Your Lester will be back, perhaps in time to start going to college next September."

"College," Pete derided. "Every buck private in the whole damn army thinks all he's gotta do is get out and go to college. And he won't never take orders from no one again. If they all get here and go to college that wants to, they'll be living out there in tents on the prairie. There ain't room in Saskatoon or any place else to hold them."

Dorothy groaned. "I've got another one. Lester, oh, Lester." And then as a child whimpered upstairs, "Annie, will you come back and look after the kids tonight?"

Pete interrupted, "Mary Ann can look after the kids tonight. Goddamn it. I'm home on furlough. Tonight Annie is sleeping with me."

The girl, Mary Ann, came with a hammer. "It was in the basement," she explained and added, wisely, "That girl's got a sailor down there. Another one."

Babies upstairs and sailors in the basement, Emily Louise practically felt Miss Freidmann shudder. There would be no shortage of news to carry back to Saint Anne's.

"Annie," Pete was objecting, "I don't like that dame living down there. There's men hanging around all the time. She's up to something and you know what. It ain't worth it, Annie. For twenty bucks a month, it ain't worth it."

"You never mind, Pete," Annie replied, sharply. "That twenty dollars Myrtle pays goes in the bank every month and it all helps. You want that wheat farm when you get out? There ain't no harm in a girl having a boyfriend or two."

"Twenty-two, more like it," Pete said, pounding the hammer against the heel of Emily Louise's shoe.

"Here," Annie demanded. "You give that shoe to me. You're drunk, Pete. You can't even hit the heel." She gripped the shoe between her knees and rapped it sharply with the hammer. "It's still pretty shaky," she smiled frankly. "You can wait for the cab and ride with us back to the car line if you like."

"No, thank you," Emily Louise walked gingerly on the repaired shoe. "You won't be wanting to make any extra stops. I'll be on my way, and I'm sorry to bother you at such a time. It's just that your landlady was wondering about her house. She's in the hospital you know. She has arthritis, it's something like rheumatism."

"Yeah," Pete put in. "Well, if she lived in her own house, she'd have pneumonia. You can tell her that, too. Tell her it's drafty and wet . . ."

"And the only thing in it that's dry is Pete," Annie interrupted. "There's really no need to worry the landlady about the house," she said to Emily Louise. "There was an attorney out the other day and he went all through the house, looking for what needed to be done. Don't pay any attention to Pete. He'll feel better in the morning."

"I'll feel better," Pete said, "when I get a bottle in my hand and my wife in my bed." He looked skeptically at Dorothy. "Do you think," he queried, "she'll have it before morning?"

Emily Louise looked at Dorothy. She was bent forward, her eyes tightly closed. Her knuckles were hard knots, gripping the edge of her chair. "I feel sure," she said, as she made her way to the door, "Dorothy will have the baby, long before morning."

Emily Louise stood for a moment on the porch, adjusting the black bandanna. As she started down the steps, Dorothy's voice penetrated the solid oak of the door, "Lester. Help me. Ohhh, Lester." Briefly, she hesitated and then continued on her way. She walked the eight blocks to the car stop and waited almost ten minutes for its arrival. When the streetcar finally came, the taxi still had not turned down to Waverly Avenue. She wondered if Dorothy would make the hospital in time. Poor Pete. A woman's world could be pretty tough on a soldier. He would probably need that extra bottle. Emily Louise found it in her heart to hope that the taxi driver had been able to find him something other than gin.

She decided to wait until the morning before relating her experiences to Miss Freidmann. No matter how gently the information was told, Miss Freidmann wasn't going to like it. She would need the strength and the freshness of a new day. So it was right after breakfast on Monday morning that Emily Louise put in the appearance at Room Two.

"Good morning, Dearie. I hope you feel strong and healthy today. I have news that's rough enough to jar you right off your sandbag."

Miss Freidmann's bed was wound up high. Her breakfast tray still remained on the table, fitting the hollow between her raised knees and her chest. Her eyes brightened and she said, sharply, "News? What news?"

"About your house," Emily Louise replied. "It's practically bursting at the seams. Renters swarm in and out like ants in an ant hill, only they're not as industrious. Let's see now. You have a lady of ill repute down in your basement and a woman with three children, four by now, has taken over your upstairs. Gin bottles," she said, deciding that Miss Freidmann might as well have a full description, "march all along the top of Mama's piano and the numbers of all the bootleggers in town are written on the wall of the living room."

Miss Freidmann stared. "You're joking."

"No, indeed. I was never more serious in my life."

"How do you know all this?"

"I was there."

"You mean you actually went inside the house?"

"That I did, Dearie. I'd tramped eight blocks and how else was I to find out what was what unless I got in. Anyway, I knocked the heel off my shoe so I had a good excuse. Although, I thought I'd never get past all the trees and into the yard."

"The man who owned the field down the road kept cows

and they kept breaking in and eating Mama's shrubs. Papa had the fence built and the trees planted. Nothing did any good though. They kept breaking in. He ended up buying the whole field just to keep the cows out."

"Do you own that field on the other side of the house?"

"I suppose so. Papa did. There's a hundred and sixty acres. But never mind the field. Tell me about the house."

"A hundred and sixty acres," Emily Louise said, thoughtfully. "Do you know what Pete said? He said that after the war, they'd be pitching tents to live in out on the prairie."

"Who's Pete?"

"The big, hairy man. If all the Canadian army ends up in your field, it would be worse than cows."

"What hairy man? For goodness sake, girl, forget the cows."

"Pete. All he had on was an undershirt."

"All?" Miss Freidmann's voice was little more than a squeak.

"Oh, pants and all that. But all he had on top was an undershirt. And he was that hairy. Hairs curling all over his arms and up his neck, poking through his undershirt. You know, I never saw so many hairs on a man."

"I don't want to hear about hairs. What else about him?"

"He drinks gin and he can't stand little children."

"I thought you said there were four children?"

"Oh, they're not his. Poor man, he's in the army and he was complaining that he never got a chance to sleep with his wife. I felt rather sorry for him."

Miss Freidmann said, weakly, "Sorry?"

"Well, not *that* sorry. But the woman upstairs, she's his sister-in-law, was having a baby. And the girl in the basement was entertaining a sailor. She apparently goes in for entertaining servicemen. And poor Pete was left all alone with his gin bottle."

"Gracious, girl. What are you getting at? Drunken soldiers. Women having babies. Some girl entertaining sailors. I'm not going to have all those people in Mama's house, turning the place into a . . . a . . . brothel."

Emily Louise laughed. Miss Freidmann's cheeks were flushed a bright pink with indignation. Pete, she decided, was just what Miss Freidmann needed. "Now what," she teased, "would the likes of you be knowing about a brothel? There's a woman called Annie, she's Pete's wife all nice and legal, and if you ask me, she's the shrewd one. She's probably making money on that rent. She has her sister with all the babies upstairs. Then she has this Myrtle down in the basement. She gets twenty dollars a month from her. Pete said so."

"I'll have them out."

"Old Dickey was right, you know. The place is in a mess. It'll cost a mint to clean it up when they do leave."

"I don't care. I'll have them out." Miss Freidmann's eyes were bright and her bent fingers trembled. "No wonder Mr. Dickey didn't tell me what they were using that basement for. I won't have such goings on in Mama's house. Now you go along and leave me alone. I want to think."

"I'll leave you alone, Dearie, just as soon as I get you dressed for the day. Here now, off with your shirt. You know, I'll bet you're a little like Papa when you get upset."

"I'm not upset. It's just that I don't see how anyone in his right senses could rent Mama's lovely house to people like that. What are you doing? You're making me all cold."

"You'll soon get warm again. I just thought you'd be in need of your false front today. And your nice pink nightie . . . Now, we'll just fluff your pillows and wind you up a bit. After all, you must remember your position."

Miss Freidmann stared at the pink nightgown cascading off the stiff peaks that rose on her chest. "Position," she said in bewilderment. "What position?"

Emily Louise grinned, "Well, aren't you," she asked and left Miss Freidmann alone to reflect upon the answer, "aren't you, after all, the mistress of a brothel?"

CHAPTER 7

Miss Freidmann lay all that day, thinking. At least she was trying to think. There was such a commotion up the hall, it was difficult to concentrate on anything. Doors banged. Feet tramped heavily. People were laughing, people were talking, and there was music of the kind that emanated from no radio.

Miss Freidmann tried to ignore the noise. Deliberately, she concentrated on the renters in her house, this Pete and his wife, Annie. And Annie's sister who kept having babies. She pictured Mama, dark haired and beautiful, her long fingers charming the melody from the old piano. And Mama's ten fingers faded into ten gin bottles, stark, empty, and ugly, sullying the polished top. Then her thoughts descended downstairs to the basement and to Myrtle. A slinky Myrtle, draped in negligee. Myrtle with a sailor. Myrtle cavorting under the furnace pipes. Myrtle. Myrtle. Myrtle.

Miss Freidmann's knees were caught in pain and the pain escaped to her toes and stayed there, nagging and throbbing. Her eyes, searching the pain, encountered her breasts. Breasts that still rose in those stiff ridiculous peaks. Myrtle's chest wouldn't be stiff and peaked.

Miss Freidmann's back was stiff and sore. She tried to move a little and felt the illusive pain twinges shoot back up her body and into her neck. That nightgown was a much too vivid pink. Myrtle's nightgown wouldn't be pink. Or, Miss Freidmann wondered and felt guilty just wondering, would Myrtle wear a nightgown at all?

And mixed in with Myrtle and nightgowns and Pete and gin bottles, there was the constant commotion from the hallway. By mid-afternoon, Miss Freidmann's thoughts were still a jumbled disorder. A pill. She needed another pill. Desperately, she pushed on the buzzer. She got Emily Louise.

"I thought you wanted to be alone all day so you could think?"

"How can I think with all that dreadful noise? What on earth is going on out there?"

"They're holding a wake."

"A wake?"

"A wake it is, my Pretty. Although to be sure, it's a bit early, seeing as she's not quite dead yet and all. Mother Superior sent word to the Pleoskis that it could only be a few more days at most. I guess you really wouldn't call it a wake. Let's just say they all turned up to give her a send off."

"It sounds like a stampede."

"It very nearly is. To be truthful, we never expected quite so many. There's sons and daughters, grandsons and granddaughters, and they've brought all the uncles and cousins. They're eating salami sandwiches and drinking out of 7-Up bottles. A big strapping soldier is there, playing an accordion and a couple of airmen are down on their haunches doing some sort of jig. And whether you call it a wake or a send off, they're really doing themselves proud."

"Where is Sister Mary Sophia?" Miss Freidmann complained. "Why doesn't she put a stop to it?"

"Sister Mary Sophia has gone and shut herself in the linen room. She's sitting there sewing tapes on all the torn nightshirts. And every time the noise gets a bit extra loud, she just stops sewing, closes her eyes, and says a Hail Mary or two."

"For goodness sakes. Don't they know there are sick people in here? We can't put up with all that noise."

"It won't be much longer, Dearie. They're all going out on the six o'clock train tonight. It's a shame you aren't down the hall a bit so I could open your door and you could see the fellows . . ." Emily Louise raised an eyebrow. "Big, husky ones, they are. If it wasn't such a sad occasion, I might even cast an eye myself."

"It isn't decent. A woman lying on her death bed and all

that singing and dancing. If you ask me, it's a strange way to go."

"Well, my Pretty, if she's sampling what's in those 7-Up bottles, it's a happy way to go."

"Surely they're not going to get her get drunk when she's just waiting to die?"

"No, Dearie, she's not getting drunk. Sure, and how could she get drunk when there's not a drop of anything can get past the rattle in her throat. She just lays there puffing on her pipe with her fingers holding the beads and her eyes on those big, strapping fellows." Then Emily Louise's mood changed with quixotic suddenness. "And I'll tell you, it's all in the eyes of her. Death, I mean. Death, burning in her eyes. They see strange things they do. I'm sure of it. They see strange things before they die."

"Goodness, girl," Miss Freidmann shivered. "You give me the creeps."

"Saint Anne's is a creepy place, my Pretty. And if all you wanted was to ask about the noise, then I'll be creeping on my way again. I have to keep an eye on Maribel. She's all excited over that accordion music."

"That wasn't all I wanted. I want you to ask Sister Mary Sophia for another pill."

"Now, you're not needing another pill. You need a good clear head to think. Just shut your eyes a minute and count the hairs on Pete's chest. You'll be all relaxed in a jiffy."

"My shoulders ache. Ask Sister for a pill."

"Oh, all right. I'll go and see what I can do." Emily Louise turned at the door. "Speaking of pills, Dearie. Chin up and chest out. Here comes a caller."

Miss Freidmann heard Emily Louise's lilting voice out in the corridor. "Good afternoon, Sir."

She heard his reply. "Good afternoon. Ah, yes, *good* afternoon."

Mr. Dickey. Surely not today. Miss Freidmann stared forward in blank dismay. She hadn't made up her mind how to approach him about the house. There was the noise of that wake going on up the hallway and she had those dreadful things on her chest. Why had she ever consented to let Emily Louise put them on her? And why didn't they make them like balloons, so you could pop them in an emergency? Did they have to stand up so stiff and firm? Why weren't they made to droop a bit in bed? It occurred to her that they probably weren't made to be worn in bed. Desperately, she pulled at the spread, only to have it slip from between her bent fingers. She clutched at it again, but it was too late. There was a gentle tap and he had entered the door.

"Good afternoon, Miss Freidmann." He stopped in the act of putting his hat on the bedside table. "My goodness, you are looking well today. Remarkably well."

Miss Freidmann fixed her gaze on her thin arms. She noticed the way her hands slanted away from the rigid wrists, the fingers, bent, claw-like, and deformed. She said, shortly, "I don't feel remarkably well."

He said lightly, "Then my news will surely cheer you. I have very good news for you today. I suppose you are wondering why I am here this afternoon. Well, it just happens there has appeared a miraculous solution to all your problems." He went on with no effort to hide his elation. "A simply marvelous opportunity has occurred."

Miss Freidmann was cautious. Such jubilation was not to be trusted. It would be best, she thought in the face of it, to pretend ignorance about the renters in her house. She said, skeptically, "Oh."

"Yes, indeed. A marvelous opportunity." Mr. Dickey's hair was thinning on the top, Miss Freidmann noticed. And he looked a little thin and peaked. Still, his speech was energetic enough. "We have found a client," he went on with enthusiasm, "who wishes to buy your house. I have told him of your circumstances and he has made an offer of ten thousand dollars. And that's the reason I'm here. I knew you'd want to act quickly. We mustn't," he smiled, "give him time to change his mind. I'm not sure he realizes the repairs it needs. Just think of it. Ten thousand dollars. Cash, too, for that old house and field."

"It's not such an old house as all that."

"Not in years, perhaps. But in disrepair."

"And it's a very good oat field. The man told Papa so."

"But, ten thousand dollars, Miss Freidmann," he said. "Think of all the extra comforts it would buy you. All the extra services and attention."

"Do you think I'm going to be here forever, then, to spend ten thousand dollars on extra services and attention?" Miss Freidmann's mind grasped the meaning behind her own words. He did think she was going to be in Saint Anne's forever. She wasn't ever going to need a house.

That old woman was dying up the hall. And the music at her wake wasn't the least bit funeral. When Miss Freidmann died, there wouldn't even be a wake. The thoughts tumbled, willy-nilly, through her mind.

"No, of course, you won't," his voice was soothing. "However, the house is getting older all the time and it's going to cost a lot to repair it. If you sell it, you won't have any of the worry and you'll have the extra money for medicines and things."

"I have money for medicine and things. I can manage without selling the house."

He said, patiently, "Of course, you can manage. It's not exactly the question of need, Miss Freidmann. There's the question of what, from a business viewpoint, is the best thing to do."

"Hmmm." Miss Freidmann was grateful for the unexpected tap on the door. Grateful for the unexpected entrance of Emily Louise.

"Begging your pardon," Emily Louise treated Mr. Dickey to her most charming smile. "Miss Freidmann asked for a pill. I thought I'd be leaving it before I was off for the day."

"Off?" Miss Freidmann questioned. "So soon?"

"I worked straight through today, Dearie. So Sister Mary Sophia said I could go and she would put you all to bed. Tonight," she added, "I'm going to have a night out on the town. I'm going to a nice cheerful movie and I'm going to forget all about Saint Anne's and the mad and the dead and the dying. I only hope that those who are going are all safely gone and wheeled away before I get back in the morning. So fare-thee-well, Dearie," she plumped Miss Freidmann's pillows and propped her, chest and all, a little higher in the bed. "I'll see you in the morning." She gave a cheerful nod to Mr. Dickey and left the room.

"Who," Mr. Dickey asked, "is that young woman? A very vital sort of person."

"Oh, she's vital, all right," Miss Freidmann answered.

"I should think she'd be very cheerful around a sick room. That's just what you need, you know. Someone cheerful around." His eyes were still on the doorway where Emily Louise had departed.

Miss Freidmann looked at him, sharply. His eyes glowed a little, exactly the way Bob's had glowed when he had looked at Emily Louise. Miss Freidmann would not admit the envy. She said quickly, "Well, she won't be here very long. Just until she pays a bill. She had . . ." Mr. Dickey was a respectable lawyer. Of course, he'd be shocked. "She had a baby."

"Oh." He thought it over. "Poor child."

Poor child? Poor child, indeed. Miss Freidmann's knees quivered over the sandbag. "She's not exactly a child."

"No," he said. "No, I suppose not. Still, it's a pity. What did she mean about mad, dead, and dying?"

"This is a hospital for the chronically ill," Miss Freidmann explained carefully. "A lot of people in here are old. They die." She added, abruptly, "There's an old woman up the hallway who's dying. Now."

"Oh," his eyes went again to the doorway. The accordion player still played on with zest and gusto. "I'll have to hurry along today," he said with no reluctance. "Business, you know. I hope you will consider this offer for your house. As your attorney, I'm inclined to advise you to sell. It's a good price. And cash, too."

Miss Freidmann said only, "I'll think it over." When he

had gone, she knew without doing much thinking at all, that she wasn't going to sell. Once she sold that house, would Mr. Dickey bother to come and see her again?

Miss Freidmann felt irritated with Mr. Dickey. He had been fidgety and he hadn't mentioned those renters or Myrtle. And then there was the way he had stared after Emily Louise and then ran off the minute he found out that woman was dying up the hall. However, Mr. Dickey came to see her and that was the one point in his favor. Miss Freidmann had not been visited for many years. There was a satisfaction in having a man, even a rather pinched up man like Mr. Dickey, come to call. He might, as Emily Louise said, be an old Dickey Bird . . . But, as far as that house was concerned, wasn't she, Miss Freidmann, being asked to feather the nest?

Rolled high in the bed, eyes bright and chest out, Miss Freidmann thought over the situation and almost twittered her satisfaction. Not for five years had things seemed to be going so well. She remembered Papa and the occasions when he had been in charge of a situation. She recollected him, standing, back to the fireplace with thumbs hooked under his armpits, slowly raising himself on tiptoe. She could see his toes denting the thick pile of the carpet as he talked. "Any fool can make money, you know. But only a wise man can keep it. And only a smart man can make of it, more. The smart man, always he makes of it more."

Miss Freidmann lay thinking. She was not beautiful, not in the least like Mama. She ought to be like someone. Perhaps she was a little like Papa. Not smart, of course. Not smart enough to "make of it, more," but wise enough, at any rate, to keep what she had. She'd be quite firm with Mr. Dickey when he returned. That house was not for sale. And when that was settled, he could just set about getting those renters out of there.

Miss Freidmann ate all her supper in her elation. The music crashed to a crescendo up the hall. The guests clattered their way down the hallway and left. And now, the silence became unbearable. She was rolled too high. Her back hurt. She tried to slide down in the bed and her eyes met the accusing points of her chest. She slid only into gloom. Sister Mary Sophia was coming to put her to bed. Sister Mary Sophia would be removing the pink nightgown, unhooking the brassiere and removing those padded things inside. Oh, the boldness of that Emily Louise. What would Sister Mary Sophia think?

Miss Freidmann never knew what Sister Mary Sophia thought. She could not even guess. Sister Mary Sophia came gently and softly. She removed the pink nightgown calmly, as though all the patients at Saint Anne's wore silken gowns. She unhooked the brassiere and with untrembling fingers, she dropped the little pads in the drawer of the bedside table.

Sister Mary Sophia's chest—if she had a chest (and she must have because she was soft and sweet and womanly—was hidden behind a white starched bib. She said softly, "It's quiet now. I hope you'll have a good sleep tonight."

Miss Freidmann said, "I hope so." She had swallowed her pill, the bedpan had been warmed, and now her knees curled comfortably over the sandbag. The pillows were wedged so expertly under her shoulders that her head and neck rested upon a soft cloud. And Sister Mary Sophia apparently hadn't been too shocked by the pads in the brassiere. How much did a nun know about that sort of thing?

Sister Mary Sophia billowed away and Miss Freidmann was glad she had not turned out the light. After the stirring music of the afternoon, there was a dreadful quietness about Saint Anne's now that it was night. She tried thinking of Mr. Dickey, but he was disappointing and could not banish the quiet. She though of Bob and found the memory fleeting. In the end, it was Pete. Pete drinking gin in Mama's parlor while Myrtle was slinking about downstairs in the basement, finally wrested her from the dreariness of Saint Anne's.

Some time later, Sister Mary Sophia saw the glow behind the door of Room Two. Softly, she tiptoed in to put out the light. Miss Freidmann, small, bent, crippled, and deformed, lay with a wool blanket tucked closely under her chin, quite soundly asleep.

Sister Mary Sophia made her way down the hall. One by one, her charges were soothed. Beds were straightened, pills were given, and one by one, the lights were turned off. And then, it was all finished except for Mrs. Pleoski, who perhaps would not live until morning. Mrs. Pleoski, who must be prepared for Extreme Unction.

Sister Mary Sophia opened the door and drew in her breath. The suffocating odor of cancer, disguised a little by cigarette smoke, still lingered heavily in the room. She began working, swiftly, breathing in fast shallow breaths. She cleansed the thin face and arms, brought the hands from under the covers, and placed them on a square of white linen. Black rosary beads were twined between the clutching fingers. She cleansed the toes and feet and put them, the skin dry, gray, and flaky, on another square of fine linen. The covers at the foot of the bed were folded back neatly, precisely. She said at last, "Did you have a nice visit with your family?"

The dark eyes moved in the wrinkled face. Mrs. Pleoski moved her lips, but made no sound.

"Such a nice family. They love you very much." The eyes thanked and seemed to question.

"Father is coming to bless you." The eyes understood. The lips tried to smile.

Sister Mary Sophia tied the stiff white nightgown as tightly as she could. It was still much too large. She pulled it higher and arranged it to cover the scars that crept up into the hollows of the neck. Still, the gown lay in stiff folds over the barren chest.

Strangely, Sister Mary Sophia found her thoughts going back to Room Two and the padded brassiere she had dropped into Miss Freidmann's drawer. There was a complexity and incongruity to life. Especially here, where so much of life was death.

Reverently, she lit the candles and placed them with the crucifix on the linen covered bedside table. Still, her thoughts returned to Miss Freidmann. Perhaps, the false breasts were a good sign. For five years, Miss Freidmann had lived at Saint Anne's. And while living, had seemed to die a little every day. Yet, Mrs. Pleoski, even now intimate with Death, appeared only to live the more.

Sister Mary Sophia looked around carefully. Everything was in order. Extreme Unction, the last rites of the Roman Catholic Church; it would be beautiful as only the sad can be truly beautiful. She paused at the door and her eyes were soft, dark, and luminous. When she had been a novitiate and taking her nurses' training, she had not contemplated the type of work she was doing at Saint Anne's. She had not realized what it would be, to work always with Death. Keeping it at bay for awhile, making it come more slowly with a touch of dignity.

Standing there, she remembered Mother Superior's words soon after she arrived. "The stone, to become round and polished and beautiful, must break away from the bank and cast itself into the stream."

Tonight, for Mrs. Pleoski, the stream raced quickly. Tonight, she would cast herself willingly into that stream. The burning eyes on the pillow were turning a smoky opaque. The pulse beat was throbbing ever more slowly in her neck. Sister Mary Sophia sighed and turned away. It was time to call Father Mullaine.

CHAPTER 8

Mr. Dickey sat waiting in the foyer of the theater that evening. Uncertain and ill at ease, he doubted his own wisdom in waiting. There was no reason to expect Emily Louise to choose this particular movie, except that it was within walking distance of Saint Anne's.

He sat, packing tobacco restlessly into his pipe, wondering if she would come and almost regretting the impulse that caused him to wait. Yet he waited, in spite of himself. The girl apparently worked constantly with Miss Freidmann and she seemed to be the practical type. Perhaps, if he worked it right, she might put in a word for his cause.

And Herbert Dickey certainly had a cause. He was desperate in his anxiety to get Miss Freidmann to sell that house and property. He had convinced himself that his whole career depended upon it. Mr. Dickey had passed forty and still the recognition, or even the mild sort of fame that he allowed himself in his less inhibited dreams, had so far passed him by. He might have been finding his fame and prestige in the army. Many men were. However, the very thought of the intimacies of barracks living left Herbert Dickey clammy with apprehension. Long ago, he had submitted his flat feet and an ancient back injury for a medical exemption.

Professionally, he might have attained some fame as a criminal lawyer or a prosecuting attorney. Yet, it was a matter of record that criminals had unusually long memories for the names of prosecuting attorneys. And often-times they had sensitive friends as well.

Mr. Dickey had decided, therefore, to settle with the long and safely established firm of Ames & Bates. Now he was setting about making his services available to as many influential Saskatoon businessmen as possible. Herbert Dickey had decided his career lay in the field of politics. And having decided, he worked with unblinking determination towards his goal. Local politics could lead to provincial. And provincial politics might someday even get him to Ottawa. The important thing was to begin locally. And where better to start than with the influential Mr. Farraday. He counted it little short of an act of Providence that Mr. Farraday should have approached him, Herbert Dickey, about the possibilities of buying Miss Freidmann's property.

For a rising politician, Mr. Farraday's influence and money could do much. Mr. Farraday could be counted on to bring many votes in return for a politician's cooperation and he might even contribute to a campaign fund as well. Looking neither to right nor left from the path he had set, Mr. Dickey had quite persuaded himself that in disposing of Miss Freidmann's property, he would be doing her a personal service. True, he had yet to go more thoroughly over her assets. There was a safety deposit box at the bank. But there was not the slightest doubt that in her circumstances she could use the money, lying helpless as she did at Saint Anne's. He would be doing her a service. And a word to the girl, Emily Louise, if she should come, ought to help his cause. So he reasoned, and he waited.

He threw all his reasons to the winds when she entered the door. Emily Louise came wearing an ordinary brown winter coat. It should have been ordinary, but it wasn't. The red hair spilled over the collar and lay with red-gold warmth over her shoulders. The coat seemed to accent, rather than hide. And as she approached, heads seemed involuntarily to turn. Men's heads. She saw him and her lips parted in a smile. Merriment seemed to crinkle the green eyes and she said, with no apparent surprise, "Fancy meeting you here."

Mr. Dickey felt compelled to explain why he was there. Self-consciously, he said, "It's right in the middle of the feature. I never go in, in the middle, do you? Would you like to wait?"

Emily Louise sat down in the chair across from him. "It

doesn't matter to me. I usually go in any old where, myself." She smiled and hoped she had acted sufficiently surprised. She had rather expected he would be there. She had dropped the hint on purpose. Perhaps now, she would find out what the old boy was up to. He could, she thought, have waited outside, but then he would have had to buy her ticket. Skinflint. She crossed her legs, deliberately, and pointed her toe down. She had slim ankles. Let him look. Two could play the stingy game.

"Doesn't it do you good to get away from that hospital?" he asked. "A very dreary place. Very dreary."

"Dreary as a tomb," she replied. "And that's about all it is. Most of them are buried, anyway. Buried alive."

"Don't you find it depressing?" He looked at her briefly and then looked away, knowing without a doubt that he shouldn't have waited at all. Being seen in the company of Emily Louise would do nothing to increase his reputation as a conservative and dignified attorney. Emily Louise, quiet, decorous and clad in a winter overcoat, nevertheless, appeared anything but conservative.

"Depressing it is, indeed," she replied lightly. "My spirits sag, and so do the bedsprings."

"I beg your pardon?"

"So do the bedsprings. The beds they have for the help. Old with saggy springs. You know the kind. When you get down in the middle, you can't turn over."

"Oh." He looked as though the mention of bedsprings was, somehow, a little shocking. He fumbled again at his pipe, lit it, and as he bent his head, his eyes encountered the ankles.

She moved her toe, ever so slightly. A man could smoke a pipe forever and never have to offer a girl a cigarette. Not that Emily Louise cared very much, but he could have offered. If he was as stingy with his information as he was with theater tickets and cigarettes, she wasn't going to learn very much. She asked carefully, "Don't you feel sorry for Miss Freidmann?"

"Yes," he said. "A very sad case. Quite incurable, I

suppose."

"Incurable?" Emily Louise dwelt on the word. "I hadn't really thought of it that way. Come to think of it, I haven't seen anyone try to cure her. Doctors only come twice to the patients at Saint Anne's. Once to sign the admittance slip and later to sign the death certificate. In between, they are all just left alone. I think I'll ask Miss Freidmann about her doctor."

He said, his voice flat and without emotion, "It's no use. She'll always be a helpless cripple."

Emily Louise protested his acceptance. "She can't just lie in bed and wait to die. She isn't old like the rest of them."

"She will, though," his tone was definite. "No future, you know. No future at all. I'm trying to get her to sell her house. I really think she ought to have the extra money. It might buy her a few little things to make her more comfortable." People were beginning to drift out to the lobby. "The feature must be over. Would you like to go in?"

Emily Louise nodded. The movie was ruined and he showed no signs of imparting any information. All she could do was sit beside him in the darkness, thinking, and finding her thoughts always stopped by his thin shoulders and that ridiculous bowler hat that he kept balanced on his knee. Irish O'Shaughnessy's shoulders had been broad and had invited her restless head. His knees had pushed close to hers, firm and strong. She sighed and her eyes were moist. Surely Mr. Dickey wasn't the kind to have a romantic interest in Miss Freidmann, or anyone else.

Was it her money, then? But Miss Freidmann wouldn't have enough. It would take more than a few thousand to hook Mr. Dickey. He was too cautious for that.

The house? Emily Louise could only wonder. The house must be the answer. Yet, there were plenty of houses just as good, or better, in Saskatoon. Houses that didn't have leaky roofs and smoky furnaces and Myrtle in the basement. Perhaps, it was Myrtle. Oh, never.

Her thoughts went on until the movie was over and the

news, it was always war news, flooded the screen. He watched it avidly. He would. He probably knew the name of every general of every army.

For Emily Louise, every plane, every ship, every battle was Flying Officer O'Shaughnessy. For Emily Louise, the war had ended a year ago, and yet, would go on forever and ever and ever. She was glad when they were outside. Glad when the night air, fresh from the prairie, put cooling fingers to the longing that possessed her. Glad when he demurred only slightly when she insisted on walking alone the short distance back to Saint Anne's.

Back in her room, she tossed her clothes over a chair and went quickly to remove a tissue-wrapped package from her dresser drawer. Tenderly, she unfolded a black lace nightgown, pressed it against her face, and then slipped it over her head. She turned before the mirror, watching her reflection, caressing with her fingers the smoothness of the silk. "You're a bad one, my girl. And it's best you be dressed in black. For shame, trying to spy on old Dickey . . ." Her hands followed the curves of her body down to her waist. "Ah, Irish O'Shaughnessy, I love you very much. I only sat with him to find out what he was up to with Miss Freidmann, she being so defenseless and all. And I'll never do it again, for this night my heart has been that lonely, I doubt it will beat again until morning. She slipped between the cold sheets. In the darkness, her fingers followed the familiar rosary beads, then they were pushed under the pillow. Her hands clasped about a tiny heart-shaped locket and pressed it into the soft flesh of her breast as she slept.

In the morning, she hurried to greet Miss Freidmann. "Guess what?"

Miss Freidmann was deliberately engaged in the process of getting up. She supervised the girl in blue who was winding up her bed. "Not so fast. My pillow has slipped and I'm too low down. There now, up a little more." To Emily Louise, she said, "I don't like guessing. Tell me what."

"I went with your old Dickey Boy to the show last night."
Miss Freidmann stared in disbelief.

"Well, he didn't take me you understand. When I got
there, he just happened to be waiting in the lobby. Trust
him not to wait outside where he would have to buy my
ticket."

"You deliberately told him." Miss Freidmann's voice
was thin and cracked as she remembered Emily Louise's
conversation of the day before. It wasn't fair. It wasn't fair.
This girl had already had a lover. She'd had a baby
and . . . and everything else. She didn't need to set her eye
on Mr. Dickey. Why, Saskatoon must be filled with men.
She could have any man. "You told him on purpose," she
repeated.

"So I did, Dearie," Emily Louise confessed. "But only so
I could find out what he was up to. I was only thinking of
you."

"Hmmm."

"I was. Truly I was. I thought maybe he'd let it slip what
he was up to, but not a word. He's a sly one. Not a word
the whole night."

"And what was there a word about, then?"

"He's not much of a talker."

"Oh?"

"He just sat and watched the show. Didn't even hold my
hand."

"Oh."

"And afterwards he let me walk all alone, back to Saint
Anne's. She added, roguishly, "I thought perhaps he
might ask me up to his apartment."

"You surely wouldn't have gone."

"Oh, I don't know. It might have been a good chance to
find out something. For you, I mean."

"You needn't go into men's apartments to find out
things for me. I can look out for myself. I'm not so sure
about you."

"Oh, don't worry, Dearie. I can protect myself. At least
against the likes of old Dickey. I'd be very strong when it

came to resisting Mr. Dickey. He wears long underwear."

"Good Heavens. How do you know what kind of underwear he wears?"

"I saw it."

"You what?"

"I saw it. Dear Mother, use your eyes. Every time he crosses his legs, you can see it. He wears garters, too. I never could succumb to a man who was wearing long underwear and garters, could you? One look at those longjohns and, well Dearie, all romance would be gone."

Miss Freidmann said, carefully, "I wouldn't know."

"And a shame it is, too, my Pretty. Every woman ought to know. At least once in her life. And, of course, being the way you are, maybe you could overlook the underwear. It might even feel warm to you. But I'm just not the type." She sighed. "It's the wicked flesh, I suppose. Oh well, for all my efforts I didn't find out a thing."

"Well, I did. And not about his underwear either. He wants me to sell my house."

"Come to think of it, he did mention that. He said he thought the money would help you out. Who wants to buy it?"

"I don't know. I never thought of asking and he didn't say. Anyway, it doesn't matter. I'm not going to sell."

"You wouldn't have any more worries about renters and think of all the nighties and things we could buy."

"I'll manage," Miss Freidmann said with determination. "Worries or not. I'm not going to sell. Papa was very proud of that house. It was our home and I'm going to keep it. Mr. Dickey can talk all he likes."

"Then you'll have to have all those repairs done."

"All right. I'll have them done. I'm not going to sell."

Emily Louise looked curiously at Miss Freidmann. Perhaps she shouldn't have mentioned meeting Mr. Dickey. Perhaps, Miss Freidmann did have a bit of a hankering for him, and her with not a man in her life and all. In any event, Emily Louise had never seen her so intent upon anything before, unless it was a warm bedpan. She said,

"Well, you think about it, Dearie. To sell or not to sell. And while you're thinking, keep your pinkies away from that buzzer. I'm going to be scrubbing and scouring this morning."

"Scrubbing?"

"Mrs. Pleoski's bed. And I'll reek of disinfectant for a week. The stench from that cancer is everywhere. I doubt it will ever come out."

"What happened to Mrs. Pleoski?" Miss Freidmann put the question reluctantly.

"Sure and the wake was just in the nick of time. She journeyed on last night. And hardly any of her left to journey on, at that. So now it's scrub, scrub, and scrub and open the windows and air the place out. We're full to the brim and I dare say there'll be another at the door by night."

Miss Freidmann shivered. "Does everyone in this place die?"

"Just about, Dearie. Not a very pleasant prospect, is it? Some just linger on a little longer than others. Here, I'll leave you the paper."

"You know I don't like looking at newspapers. It's hard to turn those big pages."

"Well, just pull it around and look where it's folded. And no bell ringing, remember. When I've got my hand in the scrub bucket, I don't like to be disturbed. I'll be back when I'm through."

Miss Freidmann, left alone, looked intently at the newspaper that was leaned casually on the slope of her legs. Had Emily Louise done it on purpose? The paper was opened and folded neatly across the page headed "Obituaries." In spite of herself, she began to read. "Passed away after a long illness," the papers put it kindly. "Died in a local hospital." Did the people of Saskatoon do nothing but die?

Some were getting married and some were being born, but they got less space. You had to die to rate more than a line or two. How many lines would she rate if she died?

Not *if* she died, *when* she died. Everyone at Saint Anne's died.

With determination, Miss Freidmann worked her bent thumb under the paper and the page turned over, but only half way. It exposed only the classifieds. Real estate, houses for sale, and two ads for development property. A good Catholic home for unwed mothers. Probably Saint Anne's. The beginning of "Help Wanted, Female" and that was all. It was all Miss Freidmann needed. Her mind had become engrossed with two words, "Development Property."

She lay, thinking and thinking. Development? Develop what? Papa would have known, but Papa wasn't here. Miss Freidmann had plenty of time, so she lay for a long while, just looking at the two words and thinking.

Emily Louise had been right. When she returned, she reeked with the odor of disinfectant. "Oh," she said, "what a joy to be back with the living. You creak a bit, Dearie, but at least you're alive. Thank the Saints for that."

Miss Freidmann asked, quickly, "Did you wash your hands?"

"Wash them? Look at them. Scrubbed practically raw. And the room still smells. Sister Mary Phillipe has come upstairs to take over now. She's got the windows wide and the March wind nearly blowing the Lord, Himself, off the wall. And she's having a go with Sister Mary Sophia. They argue so politely it's a treat to hear them."

Miss Freidmann was determined, after every encounter with Emily Louise, to refrain from asking for any details about what went on at Saint Anne's. And yet, the girl always managed to arouse her curiosity. "Argue?" she questioned. "What about?"

"It's spring cleaning time. Sister Mary Phillipe has paint for two rooms on this floor and she's determined to cover the cancer with the paint. Sister Mary Sophia says if we scrub the cancer off, she can have the paint for two other rooms. Rooms that need it more. But Sister Mary Sophia might as well give up. Mary Phillipe insists that the cancer smell goes right through the walls and all the way to the nuns' quarters and she's determined to do something about it. I thought I'd better leave until they decided what to do."

"Have they decided?"

"I'm not sure. It ended up with Mary Phillipe sending for the paint cans and Mary Sophia going down to the chapel to pray. Shhh. What's that? It sounds like the cart."

Miss Freidmann said weakly, "Not another one?"

Emily Louise peered from the door. "No. It's Bob and he's bringing one in. I'll have to help him. I'll be back in a jiffy."

"Wait," Miss Freidmann called. "You've got me on this pan."

"Well, just sit tight, Dearie. I'll be right back." Miss Freidmann sat tight. She sat tighter and tighter while the hard metal clashed with the hard bones of her hips and her back.

When Emily Louise finally returned, she said gaily, "Well, chalk one up for the power of prayer."

"What on earth are you talking about?"

"It must be the power of prayer. While Mary Phillipe waited for the paint and Mary Sophia knelt praying, in comes this poor creature and not a bed in the house but Mrs. Pleoski's. So there he is."

"What about the smell?"

"Oh, the smell won't be bothering him. He's out cold and smells worse himself. He fairly reeks of paraldehyde."

"What's that?" Miss Freidmann knew she shouldn't ask, she should never ask any questions at all.

"Paraldehyde? It's like nothing on earth, Dearie. And in here it means only one of two things. Either he's got the D.T.s or he's a raving maniac. Just wait until the stuff wears off and we'll soon find out."

"What do you mean, D.T.s?"

"Drunk, Dearie. A raging, roaring hangover."

"What if he's not drunk? Suppose he's mad? We can't have a mad man in here. Where's his doctor? What does his doctor say?"

"It's been my experience, Dearie, in the short time that I've been around Saint Anne's, that the doctors for these poor unfortunates don't put in an appearance. They do their prescribing by telephone. The man's either drunk or mad and whichever it is," she spoke with resignation, "we'll find out soon enough. And speaking of doctors, where's your own?"

"He never comes."

"Why not? Don't you pay him?"

"Of course, I pay him, but what can he do?"

"If I were you, I'd be fluttering a few dollar bills under his nose. You might be surprised what he'd do."

"Doctors push and pull at my joints. I'd rather be left alone."

"All right. If you want to spend the next forty years with cancer and mad men, you go ahead and be left alone. I'd rather have my joints pushed and pulled, myself. Besides, if I were you and had a bit of cash to spare, I'd have a doctor call if it was only to look at him once in awhile. It would be worth a few dollars to have a nice young man come and feel your pulse."

"My doctor is old and married and bald."

"Get a new one."

"I need a new nurse. Get me off this pan."

"No sooner said than done, Dearie." Emily Louise added thoughtfully as she worked, "What a pleasant place Saint Anne's might be, if only the patients didn't have bottoms. Men's bottoms and women's bottoms, fat ones and thin ones and all needing attention. My day begins and ends with bottoms. You'll never know what a trial they are to me."

Miss Freidmann said, dryly, "It's not only the patients bottoms that you have to worry about."

Emily Louise laughed. "My, but we are sharp today. You're very entertaining when you are sharp and perky." Her laugh was interrupted by a muffled cry from up the hall.

The cry came again, louder, a weird, unnatural wail. It was followed immediately by a tap on the door and Bob's voice, sharp and urgent, "Miss Emily. Can you come?"

"Right away, Bob." Emily Louise gave a quick push to the sandbag, hastily pulled the covers over Miss Freidmann's legs, and left the room.

Miss Freidmann gazed steadily ahead at the door. Emily Louise had hurried off and left the bedpan on the table, right beside her bed. Over the top for a cover, she had hastily tossed the folded newspaper. Miss Freidmann looked only once and, thereafter, she kept her eyes carefully averted.

The paper was still folded on the page of "Obituaries." And five words printed their bold message across the top of the bedpan, "Died In A Local Hospital."

CHAPTER 9

Emily Louise left Miss Freidmann to follow Bob who was already hurrying back up the corridor. He strode swiftly, not waiting as he usually did, to tease and banter. From his hand there swung several wide, canvas straps.

Emily Louise found considerable comfort in Bob's presence on the second floor of Saint Anne's. There was reassurance in his muscular, white-clad figure and in his slow, halting manner of speech. Sister Mary Sophia apparently felt the reassurance, too. She waited in the hallway, a hypodermic syringe in her hand, the needle balanced on its little sterile puff of cotton.

"I called his doctor," she said, quietly. "He said we could give him morphine."

"Then his doctor ought to be here to give it to him," Bob answered, wryly.

The three of them hesitated outside the room where only yesterday the musicians had played of life and living for the dying Mrs. Pleoski. It was a different sound now that came from behind the closed door. There was the sharp sound of breaking glass. Sister Mary Sophia moved forward, but Bob stopped her.

"You can't go in there with that hypo yet, Sister."

Emily Louise spoke quickly. "If that man's mad, you're not getting me in there either."

"Oh, he's not mad, Miss Emily." Bob opened the door carefully. "The old fellow is just a bit upset. Or senile. Isn't that what they'll say, Sister?"

In spite of her objections, Emily Louise followed Bob and Sister Mary Sophia into the room. Inside, standing behind Bob with her back against the door, she stared in disbelief. The room she had scrubbed so meticulously a few hours before was in shambles. The blankets had been tossed from the bed and lay on the floor with a shattered water jug. The urinal had been hurled into a corner. A man sat on the edge of the mattress. He was old, haggard, emaciated, and quite naked. He sat, staring at the wall while his clutching fingers found the draw sheet. He took it up in his hands and methodically set about tearing it into shreds. The white strips fluttered to the floor and joined the remains of what had, obviously, been his night shirt.

"Sons of bitches, sons of bitches," he moaned. He swayed for a moment and then with a scream, he dropped the sheet and clawed at his face. Blood traced his fingers down his cheeks.

Emily Louise turned away. Beside her, Sister Mary Sophia stood quietly, still holding the hypodermic ready in her hand.

"Come on, Dad." Bob approached the bed, his voice soft and soothing. "Let's lie down and have a little rest."

"Sons of bitches." The old man screamed it loudly, his fingers reaching swiftly for Bob's face. Quickly, as the man reached forward, Bob looped one of the canvas strips about the bony wrist. Another was slipped over the man's forearm and the two were snapped to the frame of the bed.

"Sons of bitches," the old man screamed and before Bob could raise the rail, he flung himself from the bed and crouched, cowering, on the floor, his one arm held high and tight by the straps.

Bob bent over and as he bent, the white shirt stretched tight over his shoulders. Bodily, he picked the patient up and his muscles knotted against the old man's frenzy. He raised him, kicking and screaming, back onto the bed and held him there on his back. "Clamp it," he said to Emily Louise. "Quick. Snap his other arm and put up the rail." Automatically, Emily Louise followed his directions. And then, she helped until the canvases had been fastened about the old man's thin legs.

"Sons of bitches. Sons of bitches." Sister Mary Sophia, moving swiftly and with assurance, injected the morphine. "Sons of bitches," he screamed and the canvasses stretched and pulled until it seemed that either flesh or cloth must tear.

Silently, working with Bob and Sister Mary Sophia, Emily Louise helped to get another draw sheet under the man, under the canvas straps and covering the mattress. It was soiled before they had tucked it in place. Bob fetched another and they started over again.

Sister Mary Sophia asked thoughtfully, "Is he a Roman Catholic, do you think?"

"If he is," Bob replied, "he's a very mad one."

"Shhh." She put her fingers to her lips. "You mustn't say it, Bob."

Emily Louise spoke desperately, "Surely, Sister, he'll not be staying here. He belongs in an asylum."

Bob shrugged. "Let's see. It will be two weeks to a month, won't it, Sister? Isn't that how long it usually takes? It happens, Miss Emily," he explained, "every once in awhile. He probably has relatives who will deny he is insane right up to the door of the institution. They'll insist it's just a nervous breakdown."

Emily Louise looked at Bob and Sister Mary Sophia in wonderment. They accepted this sort of thing. They'd seen it all before. There were aspects to Saint Anne's that Emily Louise found unbearable. An old man, mad and frightening, tied and strapped as her father might have tied and strapped a mad and ornery bull.

She fought an inclination to turn and run. She, too, just as surely as the old man, was chained to Saint Anne's. Chained by her penance, chained by the bill. Some part of her virtue might have been sacrificed, and sacrificed gladly, for love. What honor remained could never be sacrificed for fear.

Out in the hallway, Bob relaxed. "Well, Miss Emily, another one to feed tonight."

"I'm not going in there. Give him another dose of paraldehyde."

"There's no nourishment in paraldehyde. You wouldn't want to starve him to death."

"Death would be a release."

Sister Mary Sophia commented quietly, "Poor creature. I must find out from Superior if he is a Catholic."

"He doesn't swear like one," Emily Louise observed. Then she added, "You may be sure of one thing. Sister Mary Phillipe won't be going in there to paint that room."

"No, she won't." Sister Mary Sophia smiled, a smile which, if it hadn't been for the angelic look on her face, would have seemed downright triumphant. "No, she won't, will she? I wonder what Mary Phillipe will do about that."

They found out what Mary Phillipe would do the next day. She opened the door, she looked at the old man, and came right back out again. "I can't go in there, Mary Sophia," she said. "That man has no clothes on."

"Isn't there a blanket?" Sister Mary Sophia asked innocently.

"There's no blanket," Sister Mary Phillipe answered. "There's absolutely nothing over him at all."

"It's no use, Sister," Bob shrugged. "No control you know. You should have seen the linens this morning. Whoosh. Absolutely a mess."

"I just can't get behind," Sister Mary Phillipe said plaintively. "We are already into March. I have two rooms to paint here so I'll have to get started somewhere. The painter is supposed to be here this morning. Now look, Sister." She unfolded a diagram. "Here is the record and according to this," she accused, "Room Two hasn't been done for over six years."

"Room Two," Sister Mary Sophia said calmly, "is unscathed. Miss Freidmann has been there all these years and the paint is just like new. Now Maribel's room . . ."

"Paint can't be like new after six years," Sister Mary Phillipe's voice trembled. "It does seem a shame, Sister, that after Mother Superior has given us the paint, we can't decide where to put it. Room Two will have to be done and then, Seven or Ten. They haven't been painted for nearly five years."

Emily Louise was puzzled by Sister Mary Sophia's

unexpected answer. "All right, Sister," she was saying. "You go ahead and do whichever room you think."

Then, as she saw the soft light in Sister Mary Sophia's eyes, Emily Louise understood. Even a Sister must sometimes do penance. Mary Sophia had prayed for Maribel's room. Mary Phillipe had prayed for Mrs. Pleoski's. In the face of two such prayers, what else could the Blessed Mother recommend than an impartial judgement against them both?

"What color?" Emily Louise asked. "I hope you've got something cheerful. Room Two is so apple green it gives me a tummy ache. Anyway, poor Miss Freidmann needs something a bit cheering."

"I have one pale yellow and one rose," Sister Mary Phillipe answered briskly.

"Rose," Emily Louise said happily. "Won't you put the rose in Room Two? A real blushing pink. Begging your pardon, Sister, but she really needs it."

"All right," Sister Mary Phillipe agreed. "I don't mind which color she gets. But the painter will soon be here. You'd better get the woman out so we can be all ready to start."

"I don't know where I'm going to move her to," Sister Mary Sophia pondered. "There isn't an empty room on the floor."

"Just move her out in the hall. The paint will be dry enough to move her back by tonight."

"Oh, we couldn't leave Miss Freidmann out in the hall all day. There would be all sorts of complications." Sister Mary Sophia pondered a moment, straightened her small figure, and said bravely, "The only thing I can think of is to make up that extra bed in Maribel's room. Bob, you get the cart and help Emily Louise move her up there."

Miss Freidmann looked up with terror as Bob and Emily Louise entered her room, pushing the wheeled cart. "What's that?"

"Your chariot, Dearie. You're travelling today."

"I'm what?"

"You're travelling. Isn't she Bob? On a social call. First in years and aren't you lucky? Bob's going to hoist you in his great, strong arms onto that cart."

Miss Freidmann trembled visibly. "You're not putting me on that little narrow thing. I don't want to move." And then defiantly, "I've paid for this bed . . ."

"So you have, Dearie. But the painter is coming and you couldn't contain yourself all day with a man in the room, now could you?"

"Paint some other room. This room is all right. I like this room."

"Unfortunately, my Pretty, Sister Mary Phillipe doesn't. The apple green has to go. And in its place, a nice, rosy red. Now, I'll just wrap this blanket around you and Bob will be starting you on your way."

"I'm not riding on that thing. Isn't that what they wheel dead people out in?"

"No, Dearie. Not this one. The undertakers have their own carts. Little low ones. I never could understand," Emily Louise addressed Bob, "why undertakers have such low carts."

"Probably stack more in the hearse," Bob speculated. "Anyway, once you're dead, I suppose you might as well get used to being close to the ground."

"Don't you move me onto that thing."

"Do you want Bob to carry you all the way? Well, at that, I guess it would be more of a thrill. There now, she's well wrapped, Bob, you can lift her over."

Miss Freidmann felt herself being lifted bodily. She closed her eyes and waited for the hard top of the cart. Instead, she felt herself being carried across the room.

"Look, Miss Freidmann," Bob said. "Look out there. There are the streets of Saskatoon. How do they look?"

Miss Freidmann opened her eyes and looked down into the yards below. A housewife was hanging clothes out in the March sunshine. The wind picked up the garments and fluttered them on the line. There were sheets and towels, an apron, and a suit of man's underwear. Bob's arm was firm under her shoulders. Why did Emily Louise call him "Old Bob"? He wasn't that old. Miss Freidmann had a feeling that Bob wouldn't be wearing long underwear.

She tried to collect her thoughts. It was no wonder that women did strange things when they were held in the arms of a man. It was unsettling. And with all of Saskatoon out there, she ought to be able to see something besides a man's undergarment flapping on a clothes line.

She concentrated on details. The houses seemed incredibly small, box-like, and dingy. Who lived in them? People like that Pete and Annie? Bob's body was warm, his chest rising and falling slowly. Her weight was no effort, her presence no distraction. "Put me down," she ordered abruptly. "I don't want to be held up here, looking out of the window like a baby."

"Don't you? I should think it would be a nice change," Emily Louise countered, "to look for awhile at the world of the living. The cart's all ready, Bob."

"Ohhh, my knees. You're hurting my knees. I'm going to fall off this little thing."

"Oh, we won't let you fall. It's wider than it looks. Come along, Dearie. Off we go for a tour of Saint Anne's."

"Where are you taking me?"

"Up to Maribel's room."

"No. Don't you dare. Don't you dare take me up there with that girl."

"Sorry, it's the only vacant spot in the house."

Miss Freidmann blinked at the tears of frustration. "Please," she sobbed. "That girl's a little funny. You know she is. Please take me back. I don't care, I like green. You can leave it green forever."

"That's the trouble here," Bob explained kindly. "You get in a rut. You'll feel better for the change."

They took her the full length of the hall. They passed the elevator that clanged in the night, they passed the desk, and room after room where blank faces stared through open doors. They wheeled her along and old men shuffled past, leaning against the wall, making their way down the corridor. And then Bob carefully lifted her again and put her down on a bed, high, white, and clean against the odd tan-colored wall of Maribel's room.

"Why don't they paint this room? It needs it a lot more than mine."

"No use. Maribel hasn't much respect for paint. Have you, Maribel?" The girl sidled, grinning, up to the foot of the bed.

"Don't you dare leave me in here all alone with her. She's funny. She might murder me in by bed."

"Oh, not Maribel. She's harmless. She just likes to look. She'll go away if you tell her to. Anyway, I'll leave you the buzzer and leave the door open." Emily Louise led Maribel to a leather armchair, gave her the doll and a comb, and said sternly, "Now you stay in the chair and get your baby's hair combed." Maribel gurgled and Miss Freidmann watched helplessly as the cart, Bob, and Emily Louise vanished down the hall.

The girl sat quietly, combing and combing on the bits of wool that served as hair for the rag doll. She showed no inclination to leave the chair and wander through the open doorway. Miss Freidmann lay and watched her in a state of nervous terror. True, Emily Louise and Sister Mary Sophia came by often, but in between, there was only Maribel. And Maribel crooned to the doll and combed on steadily. It was unnerving. But, suppose she stopped combing? Miss Freidmann could not sleep. Neither could she read. She lay, her fingers gripped about the buzzer, not daring for an instant to move her eyes from the girl in the chair. Maribel gurgled happily and stared right back.

The morning, and then the afternoon, dragged slowly on. By two o'clock, Miss Freidmann's routine demanded a nap. She only lay, wide-eyed, wakeful and edgy.

At three o'clock, Mr. Dickey came quietly up the stairs. He walked down to Room Two and was greeted by white coveralls, step ladders, and the smell of paint. Emily Louise saw him and, unwilling to acknowledge the Mr.

Dickey of the theater, she slipped quickly out of his way and into the bathroom. Rather wickedly, she hoped he'd get paint on his trousers. He didn't. Sister Mary Sophia saw him and escorted him up the hall.

Anyway, Maribel would enjoy the visitor. Emily Louise confided to Bob, who was methodically sterilizing urinals, "There goes Miss Freidmann's lawyer."

"What does Miss Freidmann need a lawyer for? I should think a doctor might do more good."

"You know, I told her that, too. She has a house and this lawyer wants her to sell it."

"Tell her not to."

"Why?"

"Property will go up after the war. Everyone says so. Tell her to hang on to it."

"There's no need to tell her that. Her mind's made up anyway. She won't sell that house for love or money. I don't think even a lawyer could make Miss Freidmann change her mind." Emily Louise smiled. "I wonder how he will get on with Maribel. She might even try to comb his hair."

Bob grinned. He poured Lysol over the urinals as though he were measuring a jigger of whiskey. "Let's just hope she doesn't think it's time to take a bath."

In room Twenty-two, Maribel was not contemplating a bath. Neither did she contemplate combing Mr. Dickey's hair. She did, however, keep an envious eye on his hat.

Mr. Dickey stood, uncertainly, at the end of the bed. Miss Freidmann, completely unnerved and irritable, lay upon it. She said, "I hope you haven't come back here to pester me about that house."

"My dear Miss Freidmann."

"And it won't do a bit of good to dear Miss Freidmann me, either. I don't care. I may be penniless and destitute, but I won't sell that house. So, that's that. You can just busy yourself getting those renters out of there."

"Being put in here has been a strain on you. You're all upset."

"I'm not upset. I'd just like to know how you would enjoy being in a room all day with that girl."

"I'm sure they'll move you back soon. The Sister told me it was just for today while they got the room painted. You'll feel better once you get back."

"I'll feel better when you get those people out of my house."

"But, Miss Freidmann . . ."

"Oh, don't but me. I want them out. Aren't you getting paid to look after things? And that's another thing I've been thinking about. I want an up-to-date financial account of my affairs. I don't know what I've got and what I haven't got. And I'm sure Papa left me with something. And while you are doing that, give those renters notice to get out."

Mr. Dickey spoke rapidly and definitely. "I can't get them out. No one can get them out. There's a war on and there are rent controls. The only way you can get people out is if they don't pay their rent. These people pay and they pay promptly.

"There must be some way. You're a lawyer."

"If you needed the place to live in yourself, perhaps."

Maribel had left her chair and edged up close to Mr. Dickey, watching him intently as he talked. "Good Heavens. Couldn't they have put you somewhere else?"

"Don't you think I asked them that? All the rooms are full."

Maribel grinned wetly, wiped her chin with her hand, and ran moist fingers up Mr. Dickey's coat sleeve. He moved backward. "I'll have to hurry along."

Miss Freidmann's irritation increased with the stinging threat of tears. He didn't need to rush away. After all, he could move when Maribel got near him. She spoke in defiance, "Don't forget, I want you to get those people out of my house and send me that financial statement."

"I'll try to get them to leave," he promised. "But it's hopeless. Quite hopeless." He had got as far as the door.

"And I want that statement right away."

He was gone. Miss Freidmann lay back and the tears that had threatened a few moments before now stubbornly refused to come. "Go away," she said irritably to Maribel. "You go right over there and sit in your chair."

Obediently, the girl went back to her chair. She sat quietly, her mouth open wide in a silent expression of mirth. There was the tinkling sound of running water.

Miss Freidmann looked and then pressed steadily on the buzzer. "Just look," she exclaimed when Emily Louise entered the door. "That girl wet on the floor. There's a big puddle under that chair."

Emily Louise smiled with what almost seemed delight. "Maribel," she said sternly, "I hope you didn't disgrace yourself in front of Miss Freidmann's company."

"No, she didn't," Miss Freidmann acknowledged. "I suppose I ought to be thankful for that."

"Indeed you should Dearie," Emily Louise replied as she changed Maribel's undergarments. "Our Maribel is slowly getting trained. Sometimes, she takes off her pants and lifts up her skirt when she wets."

CHAPTER 10

Miss Freidmann lay, the next morning, snug in the comfort of familiarity. The bed was high and comparatively wide in its usual corner. Her sandbag was staunch beneath her knees. Spotless white, the spread was stiff and smooth under her twisted fingers. Miss Freidmann found the new rose-colored walls decidedly cheerful. They must surely complement the black color—dyed, of course—of her hair. Outside the window, there was brilliant Canadian sunshine. Inside, however, there was discord.

Emily Louise leaned thoughtfully against the end of the bed while Sister Mary Sophia stood just inside the door, the white folds of her robe brushing the newly tinted wall. She sighed and said softly, "Oh dear. It's absolutely impossible, isn't it?"

"Bowls you over," Emily Louise agreed cheerfully.

Miss Freidmann interrupted quickly, "It's nice. I like it." After all, she had endured much for those walls. One day with Maribel and her own room was a haven. If the walls were a bit rosy, all well and good. They could have been speckled. Miss Freidmann would have settled for anything. For the life of her, she couldn't see why Sister Mary Sophia and Emily Louise stood there lamenting. She repeated, "I like it. I think it's very pleasant. Anyway," she added hopefully, "it's done and that's that."

Sister Mary Sophia turned to Emily Louise. "I don't see how we can leave them, do you?"

"We'll be accused of Christmas decorating at Easter if we do."

"Can't leave what? You aren't thinking of those walls again, are you?"

Sister Mary Sophia smiled. "No, it's not the walls. It's those curtains. I never knew Saint Anne's had anything quite so garish."

"They look like ordinary green curtains to me."

"They were just ordinary green curtains," Emily Louise explained, "as long as they were on a green wall. Against this rosy red, they look like a wreath of shamrocks adorning a Scotch kilt."

Sister Mary Sophia mused quietly, "I wonder if I dare ask Superior for some more."

"There's some pretty pink ones in the old man's room," Emily Louise suggested practically. "To be sure, he had one pulled down and all twisted around him in the bed this morning. But, it could be cleaned up a bit. They'd look much better in this room."

"How did he get a curtain down?" Sister Mary Sophia asked quickly.

"His bed was left an inch too close to the window. That old man has an absolute passion for cloth. He's forever pulling, twisting, and tearing. He got the pocket off Bob's shirt yesterday. Bob thinks that he is improving, though. He says his swearing gets more dignified every day."

"If he's going to pull those curtains down," Sister Mary Sophia said, considering, "they could be dangerous, couldn't they? He might get one wrapped around his head. They really ought to be removed. And they would look nice in here."

"Don't you hang the curtains from that old man's room in here."

"They'll be all right," Sister Mary Sophia soothed. "And you'll like them. You wait and see."

"If one of those curtains has been in his bed, it might have something on it."

"They'll wash," Emily Louise reassured. "In Saint Anne's, everything goes to the wash. Except the patients, that is. The patients have the wash brought to them. And I suppose," she sighed, "if they are going to get cleaned today, I'd better get started."

Sister Mary Sophia stepped up on a chair and began to remove the offending green curtains. "I'll get the others done right away," she promised. "We will get your room all decked out new for Easter. By the way, Emily Louise," she added, "you won't be getting off on Easter Sunday. A lot of the patients will want to go down to Mass in the chapel. If you and Bob are both here, we will be able to get most of them down at eleven o'clock. Everyone who can possibly be moved goes down to Mass on Easter Sunday."

Emily Louise raised a red brow. "The Exodus," she commented. "Well, you can depend on us to dress them all in their Easter finery and give them a send off." And after Sister Mary Sophia had left with the curtains, she asked Miss Freidmann, "Wouldn't you like to go, too?"

"I'm not a Roman Catholic, you know that. Why should I go to Mass?"

"Apparently everyone's going. It looks like being the social affair of the season. Do you good to get out."

"I wouldn't be getting out."

"You'd be getting out of bed."

"I was out of bed yesterday and I didn't like it."

Emily Louise smiled. "You can hardly compare the company of Father Mullaine with the company of Maribel. Besides, we might be able to get you down to the chapel in a wheelchair."

"A wheelchair?" Miss Freidmann flinched and said quickly, "I wouldn't know what to do in a Catholic church."

"Pray, Dearie. Or, if you can't think of anything to pray for, then just sit and look around and listen."

"I don't want to go. I'm not a Roman Catholic and," Miss Freidmann added with determination, "I have no intention of becoming one."

"Oh, Father Mullaine won't try and convert you. He has his hands full with sinners as it is. All I want is to get you out for Easter. Just get you out and give you a chance to show off your Easter finery."

"I haven't any Easter finery."

"You have so. You have your new pink nightie, your new black hair, and the new uplift. Why, you're practically new all over."

"You expect me to go to church in a nightgown?"

"Why not? The men will all be going in their pajamas. Those that have them. Some will likely be going in their shimmies. We're very informal at Saint Anne's."

Miss Freidmann replied shortly, "I'm not going."

"Oh, I think perhaps you will. I've about made up my mind to dress you up and send you down."

In the days that followed, Miss Freidmann decided to ignore the threat. Emily Louise, she acknowledged, was becoming more adept in the handling of crippled bones. She could, on occasion, be almost gentle and in time one learned to pay little attention to her hair-brained schemes and ideas. And something much more important had appeared to lay claim to Miss Freidmann's attention.

It was a letter from Ames & Bates and "Bates" had been carefully scratched out and the name "Dickey" had been lettered in above. Miss Freidmann leafed through the pages of the account and her frown deepened with every page she turned.

Why couldn't law firms come right out and say that one had so many dollars, one spent so many, and there were so many left? But, no. Lawyers wrote figures in one column, entirely unrelated figures in another column, and they were all added and subtracted with no apparent sense or reason. And then with amazing regularity, there was an entry that said simply, "to 10 % ch." And the entry was always followed by a subtraction.

Mr. Dickey had been very deliberate in following instructions. The statement was nothing if not complete. It went all the way back to Mama's funeral and included a list of costs. There had been probate expenses and taxes. Good Lord, they'd taken a small fortune in taxes. Miss Freidmann studied the figures and fretted and fumed. And every day she started over again on the first page.

Sister Mary Sophia came back with the rose-colored curtains. As she stepped on a chair to reach the rod, Miss Freidmann glanced over the top of the statement and saw a slender black-clad ankle beneath the billowing robes. Sister Mary Sophia had a slender form, not completely disguised by the full skirt of her nun's habit. Her starched bib curved gracefully in front. What made a pretty girl become a nun?

Miss Freidmann began to ponder the Roman Catholic religion. There was Sister Mary Sophia, who must surely be the closest person to becoming a saint that the twentieth century might produce. There was Emily Louise, who admittedly was a sinner and brazenly revelled in the sinning. Then there had been Mama, who took her religion passively while secure in the devotion of Papa, who was Jewish.

Sister Mary Sophia was singing as she worked. The words were Latin, soft, haunting, and provocative. Mama had surely sung those same words many years ago. Sister Mary Sophia stepped down in a little flurry of white. "These look much better. Soft and flowery. They just suit this room."

Miss Freidmann sniffed cautiously. The curtains had a clean, freshly laundered look. The window was open a little and one of the drapes lifted, flapped softly, and settled back against the sill. The new curtains were pretty. With determination, Miss Freidmann shut out the image of the roses wrapped moistly about the body of a crazy old man. With equal determination, she left the vagaries of the Roman Catholic religion and returned to delve further into the mysteries of worldly living as put forth in a financial report.

For once, Emily Louise was of no help. "It's no use, Dearie," she said when Miss Freidmann asked her. "I never could even do an arithmetic paper. And my ten fingers have twenty holes in them when it comes to hanging onto money. I'm like my mother. Father said all she had to do was look over his shoulder at the check book and he would lose a hundred dollars. Money is not for me. Not that I wouldn't like it, mind you. But only to spend. Whenever I have a dollar in my pocket," she confided, "it drives me crazy. Knowing it's there and not doing anything for me. Not feeding me or keeping me warm. Only just staying there in my pocket and not even making me happy. So don't be asking my help with your accounts. I'd say, just keep spending until you haven't any left and then you'll know exactly where you are."

So Miss Freidmann poured over the accounts by herself. Mr. Dickey remained discreetly absent. And every day, Miss Freidmann started again with the first page.

What did undertakers do, besides wheel you out in a little cart, to charge three hundred dollars? And why did it cost an extra thirty dollars for Papa? Why was Mama's little plot of ground two hundred dollars, while Papa's, right beside her, was two hundred and twenty? Did they charge by weight? In that event, her own wouldn't be much. Perhaps she ought to buy a plot beside them for herself. Fiddlesticks! It was outrageous. Two hundred dollars for six feet of dirt to be buried in. There ought to be a law about that.

As Miss Freidmann studied the accounts, however, the rows of figures gradually began to make sense. That "to 10 % ch." entry only began to appear after Papa died. It always heralded a subtraction. It must, therefore, be the amount taken by Ames & Bates, or rather Ames & Dickey, for conducting her affairs. Ten percent seemed reasonable enough, but she noted that over the years the deductions amounted to a sizable sum. And, as she continued on, Miss Freidmann more and more admired her Papa's shrewdness. She asked for a pencil and with fingers that protested five years of idleness, she made painful calculations.

As she calculated, her fingers began to tremble even more because, by the time she reached the end of the statement, she had made a remarkable discovery. In spite of the ten percent deductions made with such regularity by Ames & Dickey, she, Theresa Freidmann, was a rich woman. Why she could have spent a thousand dollars on that house fifty times and still had her shares in stocks.

Stocks? What did she know of stocks? There were some shares in an electrical company, shares in a mining venture, and some in a shipping firm in Montreal. All were paying respectable dividends. And each dividend was faithfully deducted by ten percent.

Miss Freidmann began to feel excited. She hadn't realized such money was hers. Now she would never need to sell the house. Mr. Dickey could have it repaired. She could afford it. She'd get that Pete and Annie out of there somehow and it wouldn't matter if it wasn't rented at all.

Her knees, caught in pain, brought her back to the words of Emily Louise. Her money wasn't doing much to bring her comfort. She faced the temptation to spend. To buy anything, soft pillows, wooly shawls, any and everything that might bring a measure of relief.

And then, that part of her which had descended from Papa Freidmann pushed the thoughts aside. Money was a commodity to be treated with respect. It demanded shrewdness and wisdom or, as Emily Louise had discovered, it would vanish through the holes in one's fingers. Miss Freidmann gripped her own bent thumbs over the statement as though it were a sheaf of dollar bills.

Why had Mr. Dickey not explained that she was a wealthy woman? She excused him. After all, he was new there. Perhaps he had been ignorant as to the extent of her finances. All right then, why hadn't Ames & Bates told her she had plenty of money? They'd just been content to let her lie in Saint Anne's for five years without saying a word. They probably thought she was crazy like that old man and didn't need any money. Well, they were going to find out differently. She'd get some of that money and she'd show them.

The pain came again into her joints and Miss Freidmann sank back to despair. Show them? She'd show them what? She was a crippled, bedridden woman. She hadn't even begun to live and she lay in the company of the insane and the dying. There wasn't another hospital in Saskatoon, or Heaven knew where, that would even condescend to look after her. She was bound by a sandbag and a bedpan, and she wasn't going to show anyone anything.

With her fingers clutched desperately about the law-yers' statement, she lay and waited for the appearance of Emily Louise. And when Emily Louise did come, Miss Freidmann told her to take the last ten dollars from the purse in the bedside table to buy that robe. She knew that girl and her ideas and she, Miss Freidmann, had no intention of being routed out of bed on Easter Sunday morning and taken down to church with nothing over her chest except those padded breasts and that thin night-gown. "Get something nice and warm," she instructed.

"Must I?" Emily Louise sighed. "Summer's coming on and if Bob is going to be carrying you about . . ."

"Bob isn't going to be carrying me about."

"Of course he will be. Don't you like it?"

"Like what?"

"Bob lifting you. Those big, strong hands."

"Hmmm. Those big, strong hands always seem to get a bit too high up. Right under my . . ." She stopped.

"Titties? Oh well, Bob hasn't been married, but he knows the ins and outs of a woman just the same. You needn't worry though. He knows yours are false."

Miss Freidmann reddened. Were there no secrets at Saint Anne's? "You get me a nice, warm robe," she said.

"How much can I spend?"

"I don't care. Just get me a robe. Spend it all."

"My goodness, we're reckless today." Emily Louise smiled happily. "Well, there's nothing I love better than a bit of shopping. You realize that there isn't too much of a selection, what with the war and all. But never mind, Dearie. I'll look around and for ten dollars, I should be able to find something really glamorous."

Knowing Emily Louise, Miss Freidmann should have been prepared. She should have been, but she wasn't. Emily Louise came carrying the robe in a blue box. She lifted the lid carefully and the box tilted against Miss Freidmann's slanted legs. There was a glimpse of deep rose under the tissue. As a matter of fact, when Emily

Louise held up the garment for inspection, Miss Freidmann was aware that it wasn't really rose at all. If it hadn't been so transparently thin, it would have been absolutely scarlet.

"I love this color," Emily Louise was saying wistfully. "I can't wear it, though. It makes my hair look orange. Now on you . . ."

Miss Freidmann managed to gasp, "That's not warm!"

"Well, Dearie, I'd say that all depends on whether you're looking at it or wearing it. For anyone looking, I'd say it was quite warming."

"It's shameless. What's this white stuff?"

"Just a little decoration. A bit of something soft and fluffy around the wrists and neck."

"It doesn't look to me as though that thing gets anywhere near the neck."

"It may be a trifle low in front, but it gets up to the neck in the back. Try it. They're warmer than they look."

"You'd better take it back."

"I won't have another day off before Easter. Come on." Emily Louise was persuasive. "Do your turn good. These old men up here never see a woman unless she's shrouded in a nun's habit, or dying, or ninety. Give them a bit of a treat. I'd doll up myself, but I'm stuck with this white smock."

Miss Freidmann had the robe about her. She looked down at the bright silken folds and felt strangely sophisticated and worldly. "You manage a pretty good treat, even in a smock." She felt she could afford the compliment.

"Thank you, Dearie. And you're going to look ravishing. Wait until Bob lifts you in that."

"Where does it fasten?"

"Fasten? You don't put a robe on to fasten. You just arrange it in front so that the minute you move a leg or something, it comes open. Robes aren't for covering. They're for showing."

"Over my legs, they'd better be for covering."

"I suppose you're right," Emily Louise agreed. "It's a

122

pity. Well, anyway, your top's all right. We can leave it open at the top."

"If that thing was closed all the way up, it wouldn't come anywhere near my top."

"It is a bit tricky, isn't it? I'll bet it was designed by a woman."

"It's not even decent. And it certainly isn't fit to be worn in church."

"You'll wear it all right. You wait and see."

Miss Freidmann did not need to wait and see. She knew, protesting or not, she and the robe would be at Mass on Easter Sunday. Like the dyed hair and the padded bosom, it was inevitable.

Easter Sunday morning came to Saint Anne's with a breakfast of hard boiled eggs. Miss Freidmann found hers to be unshelled and colored a sickly green. How did they expect her to shell a hard boiled egg? Irritably, she rang the buzzer, but no one came. Out in the corridor, little bells tinkled, feet shuffled and sometimes hurried. But the footsteps all went right on down the hall and past her door.

It was ten thirty and the breakfast tray still occupied the table across her bed when Bob knocked and opened her door. He wore a polka-dot bow tie instead of his usual black and he came pushing the wheelchair. Emily Louise followed him, a green silk hankie fluttering in the breast pocket of her smock. A hankie that added more curve to what, for goodness sake, certainly curved enough already. "Happy Easter, Dearie. We've got them all dressed and wheeled down and waiting. You're the last. We thought, as our star, you ought to make some sort of entrance. Now, Bob, you be casting your eyes out the window while I slip on her robe."

Miss Freidmann protested. "I can't go yet. All I've had this morning is my breakfast tray."

"What else do you want?"

"You know perfectly well what I want. I can't go anywhere until I've had . . . I've had . . ."

"Oh, Dear Mother. The pan." Emily Louise's face reflected her dismay. "Do you have to have it now? Can't you wait?"

Miss Freidmann knew she couldn't wait. She either had to ignore Bob's smiling face and confess to the urgency or go for another hour or more in misery. She shook her head and whispered, "I must have the pan first."

"I'll wait in the hall," Bob volunteered. And Miss Freidmann was thankful that, for this time at least, her natural instincts prevailed and she was spared the indignity of having to get Emily Louise to run the water. Even before the mission was fully accomplished, Emily Louise was already busily adjusting the brassiere, the pink nightgown, and the scarlet robe.

"It doesn't exactly match," she admitted. "But, the yellow would be worse. Okay, Bob, you can come in. We are all ready."

Miss Freidmann tried a last protest. "I don't think I ought to go in that wheelchair. I haven't been out of bed and in a chair for years. I might faint or something."

"If you do, I'll have Bob pick you up and carry you back to bed. And when he lifts you, your robe will come open and you'll be disgraced forever."

Bob chuckled and the wrinkles deepened about his eyes. "Father Mullaine always sings the eleven o'clock Mass a little slower. I feel sure you will become weak and faint. I'll stay right close, so I can catch you."

"What shall I do when I get in church?"

"Oh, you can look around and you can pray a bit. You'll be all right. Now, I'm all ready, Bob. Pillows all nice and soft in the chair."

"Ohhh, don't move me so fast."

Miss Freidmann need not have uttered the warning. Bob moved surely and gently. This time, with planned determination, she kept her eyes open. She saw that Bob's blonde hair was generously streaked with gray and it was brushed back, heavy and sweet smelling with oil. His face was square, his jaw firm. His hand, as before, was high above her waist. She was conscious of the unyielding firmness of the peaks on her bosom against the upper edge of his hand.

Emily Louise steadied the chair as Bob bent over and lowered Miss Freidmann slowly toward the pillows. Her heels bumped against the chair. Bob lifted her again while Emily Louise straightened the leg rest. Still, when Bob lowered her again, her heels caught against the slope while her bottom was still several inches away from the pillows.

"We have," Bob observed quietly, "a bit of a problem. She isn't going to fit."

"What do you mean? For goodness sake, put me down somewhere."

"You don't fit. Your legs are bent too far back. Will they straighten, Miss Emily?"

"Ohhh, don't push on my feet. You're hurting me."

"Stiff as a board and folded up like a jack knife. It's no use, Bob. She can't sit on a chair. I never realized her legs were bent that much. She'll have to go on the cart."

"Not on that narrow thing again."

Bob and Emily Louise ignored Miss Freidmann's protests. She might have been a bundle of laundry. Emily Louise glanced quickly at her watch. "It's nearly eleven. We will have to hurry."

In no time at all, Miss Freidmann found herself on the cart. Her knees were steadied by the sandbag, the pillows were stuffed under her head, and she was being wheeled down the corridor at an alarming rate. Little silken wisps of the robe kept escaping the sheet to flutter like scarlet flags as they went. They wheeled her onto the elevator, the doors clanged shut, and they started down.

Half way down, Emily Louise stopped the elevator. "No hat," she said. "You can't go to church without a hat." They went back to the second floor again.

Emily Louise hurried from the elevator and returned with a little square of clean, white cloth. Once more, they started downward.

"What's that?"

"It's your hat. Hold still while I pin it on your head."

"What is it?"

"Well, Dearie, if you must know, it's a bedpan cover. But, it's clean and it's the only bit of cloth small enough and stiff enough to hold a shape. I want to show a few of your curls. I'll bet it's the most original Easter bonnet in all of Canada."

"Take it off. Get that thing off my head."

"Shhh." Emily Louise pushed her own rosary beads into Miss Freidmann's hands.

"You're practically in church. Chin up, Dearie. You're going to be the belle of Saint Anne's Easter parade.

Miss Freidmann's narrow cart was wheeled through the door of the chapel and at once she felt the awe and the quiet. Bob stopped to dip his finger in the Holy Water before he crossed himself and genuflected before the altar. Then he went behind the cart again and Miss Freidmann was wheeled in behind the last pew, her cart nudging almost up against the wall.

Her eyes grew accustomed to the dim light in the chapel, light which came only from a row of high, narrow windows over the street and from the candles burning on the altar. In the front pew, there was a row of girls in blue. Several nuns knelt quietly. There were people, outsiders Miss Freidmann supposed, in street clothes. And the seats at the back had been reserved for the patients. There were men with crutches leaning against the seats beside them. There was a little, thin woman with vacant eyes, turning her head aimlessly, her hand clutching the seat before her. Old men huddled together with useless arms and palsied bodies. And a yellow-skinned crone had spread a blanket and squatted in the aisle.

Old men still came shuffling in. They were stooped and bald, purple of face and wheezing. As they groped their way forward from pew to pew, Miss Freidmann noticed there was one thing common to them all. Each wore a figured robe over flapping, boldly striped pajamas. Emily

Louise, without a doubt, had taken part in passing out the pajamas. Turning her head, she saw a strangely subdued Emily Louise kneeling calmly alone in a corner. She could be calm. Her flaming red hair was covered by a scarf. She didn't have to wear a bed pan cover on her head.

Bob came back in again, this time pushing an old man in a wheelchair. Again, he paused to cross himself and genuflect and then, with just the barest hint of a smile, he maneuvered the wheelchair right beside Miss Freidmann's cart and left it there. Then he, too, stocky and straight of back, knelt to pray.

Father Mullaine came in then, and there were the altar boys with their red and white robes. Miss Freidmann heard the soft tinkle of bells and the resonant voice of Father Mullaine. The eleven o'clock Easter Mass at Saint Anne's was being sung.

Miss Freidmann fingered the beads. She supposed she ought to pray, but she didn't know what to say. She listened to the priest praying and to the responses. The musical chant of the Latin words became a sedative, like the little white pills, wafting her to a wondrously soothing peace.

The mood was instantly shattered as the old man beside her fidgeted and moved. Thereafter, neither the bells nor the altar boys, nor the voice of Father Mullaine could hold Miss Freidmann's attention. She looked at the old man beside her. Quickly, she looked away. Then she glanced back, again and again, and refused to believe what she saw.

Upstairs again when the Mass was over and she was, as Bob and Emily Louise teased her, being unloaded, she could remain quiet no longer. "That old man down there wasn't decent. Why didn't you close his pajamas?"

Bob smiled. "I folded them shut. He must have moved. No zippers, you know, on pajamas."

Why didn't you pin them?"

"Up here, Miss Freidmann," Bob answered, "we have a problem. The men's hands move very slow and their bodies function very fast. Can't use safety pins. Their fingers are just too slow."

"And shaky, too," Emily Louise said flatly. "Can you imagine the commotion if one of them missed with the safety pin?"

"It's no laughing matter. You ought to be ashamed. Why, that old man sat there in the chair and you could . . . you could see it."

"Now, now, Dearie. You wouldn't have noticed it if you'd kept your mind on your prayers."

"How could I keep my mind on saying my prayers when he sat there with his pajamas open, and . . . and there it was?"

"Under the circumstances," Emily Louise replied with a grin, "that would be the only thing to do."

"What?"

"Say your prayers. When a woman comes face to face with that for the first time in her life, that's about all there is left to do. Pray."

CHAPTER 11

Miss Freidmann found her self quite unable to forget that Easter Sunday at Saint Anne's. It was not, however, the resonant voice of Father Mullaine singing the eleven o'clock Mass that kept returning to her mind. Neither was it the youthful altar boys, or even the recollection of an old man with open pajamas sitting in a wheelchair. The memory which returned to Miss Freidmann again and again, with irritating persistence, was the recollection of her own heels.

The sharp pain that had coursed through her body when her heels had collided with the leg rest of the chair was forgotten. In its place there was a dull and nagging alarm. How was she ever going to sit in a chair again? *Would* she ever sit in a chair again?

Miss Freidmann pondered the questions and tried to recall the long forgotten motion of stretching her legs straight in bed. She frowned, gritted her teeth, and pushed. And as she pushed, she was dreadfully aware that her legs were not moving at all. Her knees, she could look down and see them, were raised, bony knobs. They were rigid and still and they looked as if they would never straighten again.

That same morning, Emily Louise, arriving for the morning ablutions, rolled up the bed and hurried on her way again. Miss Freidmann was left sitting in what Emily Louise was fond of referring to as "a state of grace." Alone, she moved her arm slowly and awkwardly forward and lifted the covers. Unashamed and almost clinically detached, she stared at her own body. Her stomach was flat, practically hollow. Those brown pills.

And she was thin. Good Lord, she was thin. Probably didn't weigh a hundred pounds. Her body was not womanly, it was shrunken and shrivelled. Her hips were hoisted high and in that position, with her bent knees, her feet were flat on the bed.

Again, she tried to lower her legs. The left leg, she thought, moved ever so slightly and the effort carved the lines deeper in her brow. Still she pushed, harder and harder. She was sure the left leg moved a little. Her right leg stayed rigid and immovable.

Miss Freidmann lay and looked down at her legs. She looked at the bent and ugly knobs that were her knees. And when she could bear the sight no longer, she let the sheet fall back and closed her eyes and cried. For once, she was glad when Emily Louise forgot about her and left her sitting alone for nearly an hour.

When Emily Louise did return, Miss Freidmann submitted with unusual meekness to all the customary indignities. To all the little intimacies which other fingers performed upon one's body when one's own hands refused to function. At the end of it all, she said in a voice that shook and trembled, "Tell Sister Mary Sophia that I want a pill. And I want to see my doctor."

Emily Louise's touch softened. "Feeling poorly, Dearie? Pill days are always bad." And when she went to Sister Mary Sophia, she said, "Miss Freidmann must be coming down with something. She almost looked as if she was going to cry."

"I'll go in and see her," Sister Mary Sophia smiled. Miss Freidmann was one of the predictable patients at Saint Anne's. Always after the white pills she needed for sedation, she would whimper about her joints, then she would swallow the pill of codeine and go, predictably, off to sleep. There was a sameness to life here at Saint Anne's. Miss Freidmann had accepted the sameness, on the whole, very well. She could be forgiven if, once or twice, she became a little difficult. Besides, it was that time of the year.

There was always a restlessness about Saint Anne's in the springtime. The air carried it through the open windows. The feel of wild wings beating their way to perpetuity in the north land. The call to be off and living. But those who lay here? They were too old and too ill to follow. Only the wind wouldn't let them alone. It came in through the windows, urging and compelling, pulling at their bound and restless spirits.

Sister Mary Sophia sighed. The same wind ruffled the curtains in the linen room and lay its coolness about her face. She understood how Miss Freidmann must feel. Sister Mary Sophia was surprised, however, when she entered Room Two to discover that she didn't know this Miss Freidmann at all.

Miss Freidmann's eyes were bright and moist as she reached for the pill. Her voice shook almost uncontrollably and yet there was a new demanding in her tone. "Tell Mother Superior that I must see my doctor. I must see him at once. Today."

"Don't you feel well?"

"It's not how I feel. It's just that I haven't seen my doctor for months. I want to see him today."

"I'll ask Superior to call him," Sister Mary Sophia promised soothingly.

When she had gone, Miss Freidmann only became more irritated. Why did Sister Mary Sophia have to be so meek and gentle? And why did she have to "ask" Superior? Why couldn't she simply tell her? After all, she, Miss Freidmann, was going to be paying his bill.

Unaccountably, the little white pill did not put Miss Freidmann to sleep. Instead, it seemed to lend its sedation to the hours and the time dragged on and endlessly on. It was seven o'clock in the evening before the man's heavy footsteps stopped, at last, outside her door.

Miss Freidmann looked with new appraisal at Dr. Grayson when he entered her room with Sister Mary Sophia. He was plump and bald. He looked old, insignificant, and tired. Six years ago, he had been looking after Mama when she was ill and if Papa had regarded Dr. Grayson as sufficiently skilled to care for Mama, then Dr. Grayson must be competent. Nevertheless, Miss Freidmann felt a sense of disappointment.

He said, sounding for all the world as though he had seen her only yesterday, "Well, well, Miss Freidmann, how are you today?"

"I'm ill, that's how I am. And I haven't seen you for months."

"Come now. It's not that long, surely. You know doctors are overworked with the war on and all." He picked up Miss Freidmann's hand and, looking past her, he addressed Sister Mary Sophia. "I'm getting a new assistant, did I tell you?"

"No, I didn't know." Sister Mary Sophia accompanied the doctors on their rounds because it was required of her. Her manner was respectful, somewhat below the deference reserved for a priest, somewhat above the indulgence bestowed upon the patients. "I'm sure you'll be glad of the help."

"I certainly will." His voice was tired, too. "Some young fellow from the army. I can't keep up with it alone any longer. Do you know," he was practically complaining, "I haven't even been home for my dinner yet tonight." He looked closely at Miss Freidmann's hand and pressed against her finger. "Hurt?"

"Of course, it hurts. What are you going to do about it?"

"I'll order some new pills to help the pain."

"I don't want pills for the pain. I want you to make me better."

"Yes," he spoke slowly. "Well, it all takes time, you know. We must be patient." He put down her hand and started for the door.

Miss Freidmann spoke quickly, "I've been patient. I want to get better. Do you hear? I've been here a long time and my bones are just getting stiffer and stiffer. I want to get better." And then, to her alarm, she began once more to cry.

"There, there," Dr. Grayson looked uncomfortable. "We all have our bad days. You'll be your old cheerful self tomorrow. I'll order some different pills right away."

The door closed and they were gone. Miss Freidmann

lay alone in the empty room and the tears overflowed her eyes and trickled down her cheeks. And because she had been wound down and left lying flat on the bed, her arms wouldn't move high enough to wipe them away. "You come back," she cried aloud. "You just come back here and make me well."

In the morning, Emily Louise came. Emily Louise, strong, healthy, and maddeningly cheerful. Emily Louise who could walk.

Miss Freidmann said abruptly, "Take away that sandbag, will you?"

"Take it away? Dearie, you'll collapse without that sandbag."

"Take it away."

"All right, if you say so."

"I do say so. Now get your hand and push down on my knees."

"It'll hurt." Emily Louise placed a warm hand over Miss Freidmann's knee and pushed with a careful pressure. "Whatever brought all this on?"

"That fool of a doctor."

"Your doctor said we had to push your knees down?"

"No, he didn't say so. But I'll show him. He's an old fool. A muddle headed old fool, do you know that?"

Miss Freidmann's left leg cracked and went down ever so slightly. Her face paled. Emily Louse tried to push the right knee, but it remained rigid and still. "Do you know what he did?" Miss Freidmann asked. "He stood by the bed and clucked. Clucked!" She repeated the word with satisfaction. "And then he said he'd order me a pill. I don't want pills. I want my legs straight."

"They've been bent a long time, Dearie. They aren't going to go down as easy as all that."

"Can't you rub them or something?"

"Rub them? It's not enough I spend my days rubbing backs and bottoms, now I must start on knees. Well, seeing they're your knees and haven't been rubbed very often like as not, perhaps I'll take pity on you and give it a try."

Emily Louise did give it a try. Every day she came with a tube of thick white ointment and rubbed the dry, shiny skin over Miss Freidmann's knees. The room smelled of wintergreen and the skin reddened. However, the days passed and Miss Freidmann's knees remained bent, stubbornly refusing to straighten.

Miss Freidmann's knees, Emily Louise observed as she rubbed, were undoubtedly as solid and unmovable as England's Rock of Gibraltar. And like that ancient rock, they were staunch enough to keep an entire army at bay. It was like Emily Louise to add, with understanding, that even bent knees were not without their blessings.

Miss Freidmann scorned the flippancy. Alternately, she was determined and despairing. It was a despairing day when Emily Louise had rubbed longer and pressed harder. And when her knees had given not an inch in spite of it, Mr. Dickey chose to call.

Approaching Saint Anne's, Mr. Dickey was quite unaware of Miss Freidmann's knees. His only concerns were the complications in the career of Herbert Dickey. Suppose Miss Freidmann persisted in her refusal to sell the house?

Mr. Farraday would be disappointed and he had said only the other day that if he acquired the property, he would certainly owe a debt of gratitude. Miss Freidmann must consent to sell. He consoled himself. She had been upset the other day, being moved in the room with that girl. And he really couldn't blame her. She would surely be more agreeable today. She had to be if he was going to get the good will and sizeable commission from Mr. Farraday.

Mr. Dickey worried about Mr. Farraday all the way down the street and it wasn't until he was practically at the door of Saint Anne's that his mind suddenly envisioned a startling alternative. The idea was so startling, in fact, that he decided to walk around the block and think about it before going inside.

The realization that had suddenly occurred to Mr.

Dickey was that Miss Freidmann must have almost as much money as Mr. Farraday. He remembered his own amazement when he had investigated her accounts. So, if Miss Freidmann, by her lack of cooperation should deny him the support of Mr. Farraday, then Miss Freidmann could conceivably be just the one to fill the gap.

Herbert Dickey knew that a wife was the one eventuality he had never considered in his plans. He had no wish for marriage. Married life, he was sure, would be even more intimate than army life. However, in the interests of his career, if a wife had to be considered, then as that wife, Miss Freidmann presented some very definite advantages.

First and foremost, she had the money. Aside from that, she was bedridden and with just the right oratorical approach, she could be counted upon to provide that bit of pathos quite irresistible to voters. Furthermore, a wife confined to Saint Anne's could also be depended upon not to clutter up a campaign. Or a masculine bedroom.

Saint Anne's, however, was a most disconcerting place to have to cultivate either a client or a wife. This fact was forced upon Mr. Dickey the moment the door shut behind him and he began to climb the stairs. All sorts of things could be expected to be encountered here. There was, for instance, the young woman, Emily Louise. Her vitality and worldliness left him unsure of himself and uneasy.

Mr. Dickey looked neither to right nor left as he climbed the stairs and started down the long hallway. Once, behind a partly opened door, he had glimpsed an old man, naked and strapped flat on his back to a bed. All the attendants here had certainly gazed upon that old man. It left Mr. Dickey with a feeling he was quite unable to escape. And now, whenever he encountered the glance of one of the Sisters or of Emily Louise, he felt strangely undressed and exposed.

Then, too, there was always the possibility of meeting with that strange one, the girl called Maribel, who did absolutely unmentionable things to her own body. Saint

Anne's was a trial, however, he faced it. Yet, more and more, Saint Anne's loomed as a necessity to his career. And as such, it must be negotiated.

He had an orderly plan of action and that was important. First, he would continue to try to get Miss Freidmann to sell that house to Mr. Farraday. And if that should fail, well, then he could concentrate on the alternative. He could set about cultivating Miss Freidmann's affections. Mr. Dickey frowned a little. Miss Freidmann was uncommonly sentimental about her house and any discussion seemed to increase her irritability. He decided an apologetic manner might have the most influence. That was it, of course. He would apologize for not coming sooner and he would, most definitely, come more regularly in the future.

The smell of the wintergreen was discernible out in the hallway. He knocked carefully and waited. One never knew what went on behind a closed door at Saint Anne's. Mr. Dickey entered the room and had scarcely started on his rehearsed apologies before he was interrupted.

"It's a good thing you came today," Miss Freidmann was saying. "I'm absolutely penniless. There will have to be some sort of arrangements made so that I can have some money. And I don't," she cut short his attempt at reassurance, "want a miserable ten or fifteen dollars either. I want a bank account and a check book, Mr. Dickey. You can start me off with a thousand dollars."

Mr. Dickey managed a smile. "Of course, Miss Freidmann, as much as you wish."

"I think a thousand ought to do for a start." She was a little surprised that he agreed so readily. "And I want some sort of understanding with you and your partner, Mr. Ames. I'll pay you a fee for your trouble, but I don't think it's worth ten percent just to draw a check on the bank."

"We wouldn't think of making a charge for such a service," he demurred.

"That's good," she said. "And there is one other thing. I wonder if you could arrange it. I'd rather like to meet that man—I presume it is a man—who wants to buy my house."

"Yes, of course," Mr. Dickey brightened. "His name is Mr. Farraday. But you know, it isn't really necessary to meet the party who purchases your property."

"As far as I am concerned, it is necessary," Miss Freidmann insisted. "I want to meet him."

"Then I will certainly arrange a meeting," Mr. Dickey said, humoring her, and as quickly as he could, he made his departure. Miss Freidmann, he could see, was still in no mood for pleasantries. However, he reasoned, a career was bound to necessitate a few sacrifices. Her interest in meeting Mr. Farraday was encouraging. Just the same, to be on the safe side, he had some magazines sent up from the drug store with the pencilled message that he hoped she would find them cheering. And on an impulse, instead of using initials, he signed his full name, Herbert Dickey.

Two days later, he once more appeared at Miss Freidmann's bedside. Accompanying him was a rotund and ruddy little gentleman whom he introduced as Mr. Farraday.

"How do you do," Miss Freidmann greeted the little man coolly. He looked plump and ordinary. "I don't believe Mr. Dickey has told me what firm it is that you represent."

"Firm?"

"Firm. Who do you work for? Or, who works for you?"

Mr. Farraday smiled self-consciously. Saint Anne's made him uneasy and Miss Freidmann, bent and crippled as she was, made him infinitely more so. "I thought you knew. I am a contractor."

"I didn't know, but I rather suspected you might be. What do you plan on doing with my house, live in it?"

"It's a lovely home," Mr. Farraday beamed. "A lovely home."

"I dare say you already have a lovely home. Oh well, never mind. I realize ten thousand is a good price."

"Miss Freidmann," Mr. Farraday said quickly, "now that I've seen your circumstances, I must insist that I pay all costs. I wouldn't dream of taking any advantage."

"Generous. Very generous," Mr. Dickey observed.

Miss Freidmann nodded. "The house on its four acres of ground for ten thousand and costs."

Mr. Farraday sobered. "Of course, the price includes the field. You know, the old oat field."

"It includes nothing of the sort. I've taken rather a fancy to that oat field."

"But, Miss Freidmann," Mr. Dickey intervened, "you really haven't any use for an oat field. Perhaps, for an extra thousand . . ."

"Not for an extra five thousand." Miss Freidmann leaned back against her pillows. "You know, I had a feeling all the time it wasn't the house that you wanted. Now, what do you want with that oat field? Some sort of investment property? Home sites, for instance. It's quite valuable, I should think, right up there above the river."

"Well, really, I have no plans . . ."

"Of course, you have. And actually, I'm grateful to you because I realize I don't know anything about investments and things. But," she warned, "I intend to learn. I'm going to do a lot of reading. And I have thought of one thing we might do. I'll keep the house and you can have the oat field, Mr. Farraday."

The little man beamed.

"For no money at all," Miss Freidmann continued. "Instead, I'll take half the profits. I supply the land, you develop it. And we share, fifty-fifty."

"Fifty-fifty," Mr. Farraday's eyebrows fluttered. He asked with an effort, "Have you any idea how much it costs to build houses?"

"Houses? I thought you were just going to divide it into sites and sell them."

He said wryly, "I was going to build houses. But, fifty-fifty . . ."

"Fifty-fifty after your building costs. I'll be fair."

"But, you can't lose."

"In my position, Mr. Farraday, I can't afford to lose."

He said hopefully, "Forty-sixty. I mean, if I am going to build houses and stay in a competitive position, there can't be too big a profit margin. Besides, they might not sell."

"Oh, they'll sell. Fifty-fifty. We can have Mr. Dickey draw up papers. And don't let your men touch those big trees around my house. Mama was very fond of those trees."

After they had gone, Miss Freidmann sat back in satisfaction. Perhaps, she thought, she had inherited a touch of Papa's business acumen. It would be pleasant to relate the details to Emily Louise. Emily Louise knew all about men and women and love, but she, Miss Freidmann, knew more about money. She had made a good sound deal, she knew that by the looks on those two men's faces.

She was still jubilant when Emily Louise returned. "They didn't fool me," she explained the details in triumph. "He thought he was getting that land pretty easy. Fifty-fifty should pay off pretty well."

"How do you know he'll give you half?"

"We agreed on it."

"It's all very well to agree, but how do you know he'll keep the bargain?"

"I'll have Mr. Dickey check the accounts."

"Set a thief to catch a thief, like. Remember, old Dickey brought him in. Who's side is he on?"

"Somehow I think Mr. Farraday will be honest. Anyway," Miss Freidmann rationalized, "I'm not getting a penny from that field the way it is." She added thoughtfully, "I can have Mr. Dickey draw up an agreement in which Mr. Farraday assumes all costs. That way, I'll have nothing to lose and something, at least, to gain."

"He could say there aren't any profits. Then he'd get the land and you'd get nothing."

Miss Freidmann thought deeply. Emily Louise, it seemed, was determined to see only drawbacks. "I haven't signed anything yet. I know what I can do. I'll have the land divided in . . . well, about four parts. I'll let him start on one part and if he doesn't show a good profit, I'll . . . I'll call in another developer."

"Do you know any more real estate developers?"

"No, but he doesn't know that."

Emily Louise shook her head. "You know, Dearie, all the ins and outs of business leave me cold, but you seem to have a feel for money matters like a man. At least, it's nice to know you are earning it in true womanly fashion."

"What do you mean, earning it in womanly fashion?"

"I mean, my Pretty, that at least you're earning it in bed."

Chapter 12

It was some weeks later and the Saskatchewan spring had blazed into a full Saskatchewan summer. The birds mated and nested and became middle-aged and worried. Heat waves shimmered from the pavements and crept up the walls and through the windows of Saint Anne's. Emily Louise's hair clung in moist red curls to the nape of her neck. Only Miss Freidmann, taking a peppermint from the sack on the bedside table, seemed cool as she lay bathed in the soft luxury of a new pale green nightgown. It was another of Emily Louise's selections, filmy, lacy, deliciously cool.

Miss Freidmann sucked gently on the mint and reflecting, realized that her life had changed with the advent of the peppermints. Many weeks before, Mr. Dickey had deposited the money to start her bank account. And slowly, ever so slowly, Miss Freidmann had learned to spend. Cautiously, of course, because that was decreed by her ancestry. And the first sack of mints had been purchased only in self defense. Self defense against the unappetizing conditions and odors of Saint Anne's that came barging in on the vivid descriptions of Emily Louise.

"That old man in Ten has gangrene. Glory be, what a stench."

"The mad one was in a mess. You should have seen him, Dearie. All over everywhere."

Or, with her nose turned upward, "There's nothing on Earth can reek like cancer. Absolutely nothing."

So when, despite closed doors, Saint Anne's insisted on pushing its way into Room Two, Miss Freidmann had, in defiance, sent out for the mints. Long ago, Mama had kept a bowl of mints on the sideboard and they were remembered as a symbol of genteel refinement. Saint Anne's was neither genteel nor refined.

The mints had been only the beginning. There had

followed other luxuries. Little luxuries, for the daughter of Papa Freidmann must still be bound by caution.

The war with Germany had ended. Soft tissues and hot water bottles had found their way back into the shops, and from the shops to the table of Room Two. There was a soft woolen shawl to tuck about her shoulders as she was propped up in bed. And along with the pale green nightie, there had come fluffy slippers to warm—and hide—her twisted toes.

All these things came to Theresa Freidmann with the coming of the mints. And they came with the eager aid of Emily Louise. It was Emily Louise who had located the detailed street map of Saskatoon. "I just walked in and asked this nice old fellow in the garage down the way."

It was Emily Louise who made sure that every morning the daily paper was folded just right, across the section of classifieds. "Your knees, Dearie, make the best reading rack in all Saint Anne's." And it was Emily Louise again, who made sure the map was unfolded and ready for study. "I'll bet you know every red light district in Saskatoon."

As the days passed, Miss Freidmann did come to know just about every district in town. And she learned it all with the street map and the daily paper. She knew which were the desired streets and which were avoided. She knew where people preferred to live and where they didn't. Because she studied every day and because she seemed to have a remarkable ability for such things, she knew what any house on any particular street might be expected to be worth.

Once or twice, just to test her knowledge, she had Emily Louise help her by reading an advertisement describing a house and its location. Miss Freidmann would try to guess the price. She found she could estimate them very well indeed.

It was necessary, she had decided, to know the city in which one lived. On an impulse one day, she had Mr. Dickey buy her three vacant lots that were for sale in a rather out of the way district.

Mr. Dickey tried to dissuade her. "Theresa," he said (he had taken to calling her Theresa of late), "you don't need any land. You still have three quarters of an oat field." Then, a few weeks later, he appeared with an offer of one hundred and fifty dollars more than she had paid for them. "You'd better take it," he said. "It's a good profit and a quick one."

Miss Freidmann, however, had no intention of taking it. "They aren't for sale yet," she said. "I have a feeling they'll go higher."

Miss Freidmann had but a few distractions to keep her mind from her calculations. There was an occasional raid by the irrepressible Maribel who had once, on a dust mopping detail, discovered the presence of the mints. And whenever Maribel came and put her fingers in the sack, Miss Freidmann ended up by sending her away with the entire contents. She'd seen Maribel all wet in that leather chair and she had no intention of eating a mint that had been in contact with those fingers.

Aside from Maribel, there were the more and more frequent visits of Herbert—he insisted she call him Herbert—and an occasional word or two with Bob. Bob was not as refined as Herbert. He had no distrust for lawyers as did Emily Louise. And Bob shared a common interest with Miss Freidmann. That was her passion for real estate.

"House down the street went for five thousand the other day. Couldn't have got three for it this time last year," he volunteered, his head thrust just inside her door. And on another occasion, "If you've got any lots, you'd better hang on. They seem to be moving fast right now." And Miss Freidmann smiled and nodded her head in agreement. She admitted at times that she rather enjoyed the little repartees with Bob. And she liked to be called upon by Herbert.

However, the very next time that Emily Louise floated by, she dismissed all such thoughts. She was bent and crippled and ugly and there wasn't a bit of sense, in her condition, to be mooning about over men like a schoolgirl. Real estate, money, and investments were the challenge for her, where bent limbs were no great handicap. The mind was what counted.

So the summer came, and despite the sluggish heat, there was a new air of accomplishment about Room Two. And then one morning, when the sun beat with more than its usual intensity upon the brick walls of Saint Anne's, another gentleman knocked quickly, opened the door, and walked into Miss Freidmann's limited domain.

He announced quietly, "I'm Doctor Myers, Doctor Grayson's new assistant. I'll be looking after you from now on." He waited until Sister Mary Sophia had entered the room and then he closed the door behind her.

Much later, Miss Freidmann awoke screaming. "Don't. Leave me alone. Don't hurt me."

"Shhh." Emily Louise, who had been waiting beside her, moved forward. "Shhh. No one's going to hurt you, Dearie. You had a hypo and I hope you don't have any more. You've been snoring for two hours."

"I want to see Superior. Ohhh, I'm going to be sick."

"Well, here's the little pan, Dearie, so keep your head turned. If you'll just lie still and take a few deep breaths, it will pass away. Sometimes morphine does that."

Miss Freidmann did as she was bidden and the color came slowly back to her cheeks. "I won't have that doctor back here again. He nearly killed me. He just came from the army and . . . What are you doing?"

"Well, my Pretty, you are to lay and toast under the heat lamp. And after that, you get your joints massaged."

"Don't touch me. Don't you touch one of my joints."

"Doctor's orders."

"He's no doctor. He's a butcher. I tell you, he nearly killed me. He pushed my knees and my elbows and all the time he kept talking to Sister Mary Sophia about soldiers getting their legs and arms blown right off and not making half so much fuss. What does he expect? Then he told me I wouldn't have got half so bad if I had exercised. How could I exercise? He's mad. Won't that thing burn me?"

"It won't get that close."

As Miss Freidmann's flesh warmed and reddened under the lamp, Emily Louise began to rub. Around and around, over the ankles and over the knees.

Can't you put some covers on me? I'm practically naked."

"Like a plucked chicken, Dearie."

"And my head's spinning."

"It's the hypo. Have a little nap while you roast."

Sister Mary Sophia appeared in the doorway with the hypodermic syringe in her hand again.

"What's that? I don't want any more of those things. I'm still sick from the last one."

"This," Sister Mary Sophia said quietly, "is gold. Gold salts. Doctor Myers wants to try it and see if it will reduce the swelling."

"I don't want that doctor or his gold salts, not a whole gold mine. If he dares to come here again . . ."

"You'd better get it over with," Sister Mary Sophia said as Miss Freidmann flinched under the needle, "because he is coming back again. He will be here tomorrow."

"It looks as though you are going to be valuable, Dearie," Emily Louise consoled as she resumed her rubbing. "Gold coursing through your veins."

"It won't be so bad next time," Sister Mary Sophia reassured as she left. "He won't have to examine you so thoroughly tomorrow."

"He's just experimenting," Miss Freidmann complained. "He said as much. He said he didn't know if anything would help. Well, he can do his experimenting on someone else."

"You heard what Sister said. He's coming back tomorrow. Next time he experiments, you'd better remind him to put your nightgown back. You were almost indecent."

"He's mad," Miss Freidmann said. The massaging was soothing and the spinning sensation in her head was leaving. "Absolutely mad. You should have seen all the things he did to me. He looked at my teeth and my eyes and my ears and my throat and . . . and everything. Some of the examinations he did had nothing to do with arthritis."

"Doctors nowadays are very thorough. They go from top to bottom. Especially bottom."

Miss Freidmann blushed. "Ridiculous. And Sister Mary Sophia standing there. I don't know what she was thinking."

"Probably thanking the Saints that she wasn't in bed with arthritis."

"He said he didn't know if any treatment would help. And do you know what else he said? If my legs don't straighten up, he might have to break them."

"No wonder they let him out of the army. Can you imagine a doctor who goes around breaking all his patients legs? Anyway, he's young. Is he married?"

"If he is, he ought to be ashamed to face his wife. I still don't see what those examinations have to do with arthritis."

"I read once," Emily Louise stated flatly, "that gonorrhea sometimes will cause arthritis. So he was probably just checking. They are always checking. When I was having my baby, they were watching me all the time. The doctors have a great distrust of girls who have babies out of wedlock. They checked me every month."

"You don't mean he will do that every month?"

"Not likely. Not here. If you're pure now, you're not apt to get corrupted at Saint Anne's. All he will do now is hold your hand and feel your pulse and send you a bill every month. But never mind, Dearie. He's nice to look at so it will be worth it."

Emily Louise's predictions to the contrary, Doctor Myers did not arrive simply to feel Miss Freidmann's pulse and send her a bill every month. Doctor Myers was proving much more persistent. He had a wife. He confided that to Miss Freidmann as he pushed with more than usual firmness upon her knees. He also had two children. She learned that as he pulled the sandbag from under her knees and ordered it taken away forever. He shook his head over her right knee. He was dark and intense and his mouth had a tendency to pucker and turn down. "It doesn't look as though it's going to loosen up. Too bad."

"You're not going to break it?"

"I may have to." Then, seeing her alarm, he added curtly, "Look here, you can't want to spend the rest of your life with your legs curled up like this. I won't let you. Soldiers with no legs at all are walking down those streets. Right out there below you, they're walking. I intend to get you out of that bed and, if there's no other way, I'll break your legs and straighten them in casts. But, we'll try the gold for a few months first, so you needn't worry."

Miss Freidmann did worry. What else did he expect her to do except worry? How would he like it if someone came along threatening to break his legs? Desperately, she tried to move her knees. She had Emily Louise try, but they seemed to straighten not at all. Her fingers, however, seemed to be improving, and certainly something should. Doctor Myers did nothing by halves. Vitamins and milk appeared on every meal tray. Gold was pumped into her flesh and a dentist appeared and extracted one of her teeth. All parts of her body, Miss Freidmann had come to realize, had become vulnerable. Still, writing was easier and the map seemed to unfold more readily in her hands.

She had spent several days thoughtfully studying one particular section of the map before she said at last to Emily Louise, "I wonder if I could get you to do something for me the next time you have a day off."

"Next week, my Pretty. And always at your service. Now, what will it be. A pair of step-ins or a new uplift?"

"I want you to go out to the cemetery."

"Dearie. I run all your errands, and gladly, but a cemetery? Is it really necessary? They're such depressing places. All those dead souls rustling about, fluttering in the grass and moaning in the tree tops. A cemetery, if you don't mind my saying so, is such a dead place."

"I need someone to go out there and Mr. Dickey wouldn't be any good at anything like that."

"I'll agree with you there. If old Dickey's trousers brushed up against one gravestone he'd be done for. And seeing it's for you, I'll go next week. It shouldn't be too creepy as long as it's summertime and daylight. What is it now you're wanting at the cemetery? Flowers for Mama and Papa?"

"Yes," Miss Freidmann said. "You can take some flowers and put them on the graves."

"What kind?"

"Just whatever you think. I'll give you the money. And while you're there, I want you to look around. I don't remember exactly what it was like and I'd like to know. It seems to me it was just a small cemetery, a little square plot at the bottom of a hill." Miss Freidmann gave Emily Louise ten dollars to buy the flowers and waited.

The report, as usual, was vivid. "A nice little place, Dearie, and quite well kept up. Gravel paths and nice, neat headstones. Lots of trees planted about, but wouldn't you know? Gophers burrowing everywhere. I should think they'd keep gophers out of a graveyard. When I'm dead, I don't want those creatures tunneling in and out of my bones."

Miss Freidmann shivered and asked quickly, "It isn't very big, is it?"

"Not very," Emily Louise agreed. "Someone is building a row of houses between it and the car line. I'd never want to live in a house next to a cemetery, would you? Still, I suppose it has its advantages. Not far to take you when you die."

Miss Freidmann interrupted. "Isn't there a hill, well not a hill exactly, but a sort of rise behind the cemetery? Are there any houses built up there?"

"Nothing like that, Dearie. Just a nice bare hill with a few rocks and poplars. They'll never build houses up there. Can't you just imagine the ad? Modern home, beautiful view overlooking the cemetery."

Miss Freidmann smiled. "You know," she confided, "we've just found this out in time. Mr. Dickey will be here tomorrow."

"Hasn't old Dickey been a bit more attentive lately?"

Miss Freidmann reddened. "I hadn't noticed."

"Hadn't noticed? He comes trotting up those stairs twice a week and you pretend not to notice. You'd better watch him. Has he tried to kiss you yet?"

"Really," Miss Freidmann gasped.

"Well, don't let him get to that stage, at least not until you get another hairdo. The gray is beginning to show again."

Miss Freidmann remembered the gray hair the next day when Herbert Dickey called because he did stand close to the bed. She'd have to have another package of that dye. One thing, though, he wasn't paying any attention to her hair today. She was sure of that.

"You can't want to buy more property," he was saying. "What can you possibly do with it, Theresa? And property that close to a cemetery is practically worthless." And then, persuasively, "Look, Theresa, you are new at investments. Why don't you let me advise you?"

"Herbert," Miss Freidmann said firmly, "I want that property. Now you go and buy it for me and don't stand here haggling. Just get me the deed."

Mr. Dickey was back in a few days, his shoulders sagging. "A dreadful price. Five thousand dollars, Theresa. And all you get is a hill overlooking a cemetery. It's just a left over piece of land. Not even a hundred acres. And he wouldn't divide it. All or nothing, he said, and five thousand dollars."

"Cheap," Miss Freidmann smiled. "It is, really. I'd have paid twice that much."

"But why? What can you ever do with it?"

"Keep it for a few years. Then, I'm going to sell it to that man who owns that cemetery. Just think, a little more than fifty dollars an acre and he charges two hundred and fifty dollars every six feet. Herbert, how many people could you bury, allowing for paths and things, on an acre of land?"

"Oh, Good Lord, Theresa. How could you get such a notion? And what makes you think he will buy it for his cemetery?"

"He will have to. It's just a matter of time. And at the rate people die around here it shouldn't be a very long time either."

"He might start another one somewhere else."

"It would cost more. Besides, it would be more trouble. Zoning laws and all that. You know you can't start in burying people just anywhere, Herbert. There are all sorts of restrictions. I've been reading all about them. I'm surprised he never thought of buying it himself. But, people are very improvident. I remember Papa saying that. And he always said the only time to buy a bargain was when it was there. You know, Herbert, it's rather stimulating to spend money. A little like gambling I suppose."

"Stimulating?" Mr. Dickey said. "To buy a cemetery?"

"Very," she replied. "And, Herbert, the war's over now, you know. Have you done any more about getting those renters out of that house? I should think you could soon get them to move."

"The woman has left from the basement." He imparted the information nervously.

"She has? That's wonderful, Herbert." Miss Freidmann beamed. "Now, I'll tell you what we'll do. We'll have that basement filled up with coal."

"Coal? In that apartment? It would be a shame. I mean, it's quite comfortable, Theresa."

She looked at him sharply. "It must have been. Well, you can get sacked coal. That won't be so messy. But, get it there quickly before someone else moves in."

"All right, Theresa. Whatever you wish." Awkwardly, he took her hand. It was proving difficult to court a woman like Theresa. He supposed it would be difficult to court any woman. Her fingers were cold and hard against his hand. He looked down at them, curled and bent, and patted them, not knowing what else he could do. "You must get lonely here."

"Not really, Herbert. People are in and out all the time."

"I should come more often. Would you like me to come more often, Theresa?"

"That would be nice, Herbert," she said and was not surprised, after he left, to see the bouquet of roses delivered to her room.

Emily Louise brought them in. "Roses," she said. "Red roses. And the card says, 'From Herbert.' Dear Mother, he's getting bold."

Miss Freidmann said shortly, "You've no business looking."

"Well, it's right there in the open. Showing its little message for all to see. 'From Herbert.' Funny he didn't add, 'With Love.'"

"He was a little upset," Miss Freidmann confided, "because I bought that property up by the cemetery."

"I'm a little curious myself as to why you wanted to buy property like that."

"I'm going to sell it to that cemetery man for his graveyard someday. But, poor Herbert. He just doesn't understand."

"I shouldn't think he would. It must be hard to send flowers to a woman who goes around buying graveyards."

"What's wrong with buying a graveyard? It should turn out to be a pretty good business proposition. But, you can't explain things like that to Herbert. We just don't see eye to eye about my investments."

"Well, you must admit, it isn't the most attractive spot in Saskatoon. Still, I don't see eye to eye with your Herbert's investments either."

"I didn't know he had any investments."

"Oh, indeed he has. He's a shrewd one. And if you're not careful, for five dollars worth of roses, he's going to have an investment in you."

Chapter 13

In August, Miss Freidmann's right knee went down. Emily Louise noticed it one day as she rubbed. "I'm sure your knee moved. Hang on while I try a little push. There, it went down a bit, see?"

"I don't see, but I feel," Miss Freidmann complained. "You and that Doctor Myers would make a good pair."

"That we might, Dearie," Emily Louise agreed cheerfully. "But, he's married. Doctors always are. Some girl always latches on to them on the way up. Oh well, I never could be a doctor's wife. I shouldn't want my husband spending all his days looking at other women's knees and . . . things. If I was going to marry a doctor, I'd look out for an eye, ear, nose, and throat man, myself. And as long as you have that doctor working about your knees, I should think you'd wear some panties. A bit of lace would do wonders."

"I don't need lace panties. I need good heavy cotton bloomers."

"I could get you a pair of Maribel's. Nice tight elastic in the legs."

Miss Freidmann gave up the idea. "They'd be too awkward in bed," she said. "Besides, it's not so bad. Sister Mary Sophia folds the covers up from the foot of the bed."

"What a nice doctor we have. He doesn't pull the covers down, he just has them rolled up from the bottom instead. Protecting your modesty and virtue."

"Doctor Myers hasn't the slightest regard for either modesty or virtue."

"He *is* a bit on the dedicated side. But, you must admit, he's progressive. There's another new order on your chart."

"Oh?"

"You're to sit up."

"I can't sit up. I don't fit in the chair. We went through

all that before."

"You are to sit, so he has written, on the edge of the bed."

"What about my legs?"

"I don't know. I suppose they'll just have to curl under the edge."

So, Miss Freidmann sat on the edge of the bed. She sat neither willingly nor well. Rather, she sat, Emily Louise insisted, like a worried little bantam hen just starting to nest and looking as though she was ready to fly the coop at any time. And as she sat, Emily Louise stood before her to steady her, with one cool hand pushed right underneath the uplifts. Daily, she volunteered her comments.

"I have to stand here and hold you because if you fainted with your legs bent under like that, you'd be sure to topple right over on your face. You know, your precious Doctor Myers calls this therapy. And it's happy I am that he has the care of no more of the patients at Saint Anne's. If he did, we'd be needing half a dozen more pairs of hands. And in the name of therapy, we'd probably be taking Maribel downtown on a lead and playing jazz to the old boys in Eight."

Miss Freidmann sat and suffered. She did not, however, suffer in silence. "My head's spinning. I know I'll faint. Let me lie down. You must let me lie down."

The first few times she had been left exhausted. Then, there came an afternoon when she looked past Emily Louise's red hair and out the open window. And once, with her bent arm braced firmly against the bedside table, she sat for a moment alone.

The next week Doctor Myers announced vigorously, "Now we'll have to get you up in a chair."

"I can't," Miss Freidmann spoke quickly. "We tried it once before. My heels hit the leg rests on the wheelchair."

"That's what comes of lying in bed and letting yourself get all crippled like that. I'll have a seat made to protrude forward from the leg rest. You *are* going to get out of that bed."

"The chair," Emily Louise observed when she heard,

"means Bob. We'll have to dress up pretty."

"There's no need to dress up pretty. I'm not trying to catch Bob."

"Perhaps not. But if you faint, he has to catch you. You ought to think of him. Besides, you know it's going to be a thrill to be held again in Bob's great, strong arms. You don't have to be in condition to think, Dearie. Come now, isn't Bob more romantic than your old Dickey boy?"

"What's wrong with Herbert? He's a good companion."

"Oh, Glory. When a man's lifting you in and out of bed, you don't exactly want him to be a companion. It's beauty and muscles that count." And later, when she came with the remodelled wheelchair and arranged the pillows and the blanket, she said slyly, "I just hope he squeezes you so tight you squeal."

If Miss Freidmann was flustered when Bob arrived, it was all the fault of that girl and her outrageous ideas.

Bob lifted her casually and easily. "Your legs," he said, "are bent just right for carrying. And you are as light as a feather. I'll bet you don't weigh a hundred pounds. Well, some of our old girls need a block and tackle to hoist them, don't they, Miss Emily? You are a nice change."

Despite Doctor Myers' remodelled wheelchair, Miss Freidmann had to be twisted sideways before she could sit in it at all. Her weight, all hundred pounds of it, was on one thin buttock and it didn't feel feather-like at all. However, the sideways position kept her in better balance. She didn't feel like falling forward as she did when she sat on the edge of the bed.

Emily Louise tucked the blanket and the pillow firmly against Miss Freidmann's back. "Doesn't she look bright and perky, though?"

"Very good," Bob agreed. "We ought to wheel her out in the garden."

"With all the halt, lame, and blind?" Emily Louise questioned. "To say nothing of the slightly mad. We wouldn't dare leave her—so ravishingly beautiful—out there."

"Perhaps her gentleman friend will come and wheel her out," Bob said. "We'll just put her over by the window for a start."

Emily Louise took issue with Bob as soon as they closed the door of Room Two behind them. "Why did you want to suggest old Dickey taking her out for a walk? Why don't you take her yourself?"

"Me?" Bob questioned in surprise.

"You," Emily Louise insisted. "There she is, poor woman, been in that bed for years. Not a man to pay her any attention. It would do her good."

"What's the matter with her lawyer?"

"He's wishy-washy, that's what. After all this time, she deserves a bit of excitement. And you could show him up, too, being big and husky like."

"Miss Emily," Bob said, his eyes wrinkling, "lots of young men are leaving the army. Some of them are well-trained orderlies. Bob, the Swede, is hired for his strength and his willingness and he is not going to lose his job because he spent his time wheeling a crippled woman patient up and down in the garden."

"Just the same," Emily Louise was insistent, "I don't think she should get involved with old Dickey."

Bob's voice became more serious. "She isn't involved."

"How do you know?"

"Miss Emily," he said, "some things a man knows," he touched his forehead, "right here. Miss Freidmann likes men. Maybe they are even exciting. But she is practical, she won't become involved. Not at all. Now you, you are different."

Emily Louise looked steadily at Bob. The rolled up sleeves of his shirt accented the strength of his arms and the white pants hugged his thighs. And Bob was aware of her, as he was of all women. They were quite alone in the linen room. "Don't you dare," she said flatly.

He shrugged and smiled. "Miss Emily, you are as safe with me as if you were wearing Sister Mary Sophia's robes." Lightly, his hand touched her shoulder.

"I thought I was."

"If I kissed you, it would be just a kiss. No more than that."

Emily Louise looked at him and the eyes that met hers held an admiration that was genuine and kind. She accepted the admiration, knowing there was no need to repay. Gently, she brushed his hand from her shoulder. "Well, we won't push our luck. We'll just love each other from a distance. And I still think you ought to be showing some of your charm to Miss Freidmann and show up old Dickey a bit."

"When I lift her out tomorrow, I'll give her an extra squeeze," he promised. "But I'm sure, just as I'm sure the mad one screaming up the hall needs another dose of paraldehyde, that Miss Freidmann will never be taken advantage of by Mr. Dickey or any other man. So don't you go worrying about that."

Emily Louise felt a certain relief at Bob's words. Certainly, he had correctly guessed her own emotions. He was probably just as correct about Miss Freidmann's. Anyway, some men seemed to have an uncanny knowledge about women. As Irish O'Shaughnessy had known instinctively she was his for the taking, so Bob had known just as instinctively, that she wasn't. He was probably right about Miss Freidmann, too. And if Miss Freidmann was completely in charge of the situation, then it was a situation much more to Emily Louise's liking. She discarded her alarm and substituted a lively tolerance. And despite it all, stuck to her original conclusion, that a little obvious comparison between Bob and Herbert Dickey wouldn't do any harm at all.

So, in those late summer days, Miss Freidmann found her life unusually preoccupied by men. First, there was Herbert. Herbert came often and once or twice he held her hand. He was always a gentleman, irritatingly so at times, but intellectual and polite.

Then, there was Doctor Myers. Doctor Myers, who could never forget that he had been sent back to Canada with the first load of casualties from the beaches of Normandy. Who never apologized for outrageous bills, twice as high as those of Doctor Grayson. And who once, in a rare moment of confidence, had admitted that just as soon as he had enough money, he intended to take a post graduate course in rehabilitation.

Miss Freidmann knew that Doctor Myers regarded her only as a progress case to be noted and used for a statistic. Someone to be pushed, prodded, scolded, and somehow, all the while encouraged. He was the one man whom she did not like. Yet, she obeyed him implicitly because she felt if she didn't, all the amputee soldiers in Canada would arise as one body to wave the stumps of their severed limbs in scorn.

She grew to know the meaning of every furrow across his thin, intense brow. And she learned to bite her lip when he pushed and tried to flatten her joints, because if that fool of a doctor thought it was easier to have a limb curl up and die by inches than it was to get it shot off in one quick moment, then no amount of moaning and groaning would do any good. She'd just have to pay his bills promptly and hope he would soon save enough money to go away somewhere and study.

And then there was Bob, who came to get her out of bed and on her first day outside, lifted the wheelchair down the step to the garden. Bob, white-suited and immaculate, stealing a few quick puffs on a cigarette. She admitted to herself that she rather enjoyed Bob. However, the enjoyment was spoiled because she was not in control. Bob disturbed her and Miss Freidmann felt that Bob knew much more about disturbing emotions than she. That was why, despite the excitement and despite Emily Louise's urging to the contrary, Miss Freidmann felt more comfortable in the presence of Herbert. Emotionally, Herbert, poor creature, was even more inexperienced than she. She was glad when Bob took her down and then walked away, leaving her alone in the garden.

It was only ten in the morning, but the day was going

to be hot. Flies buzzed lazily. A small breath of wind pushed about her neck and under her hair. Miss Freidmann frowned and moved to pull the shawl about her shoulders. What was Doctor Myers thinking about? She'd catch cold out here.

Across the street, young girls skipped on the sidewalk. Young girls, scantily clad, bronzed legs bare to the sun. Miss Freidmann felt the heat of it on her own head. Her eyes squinted against the unaccustomed glare. She watched the shade ripple under the branches of a poplar tree and the sun warmed the blanket tucked about her knees and sank its heat into her hands.

She closed her eyes and still the light pushed its way under her lids. It had been five years. Five years since the sun and the wind had touched her skin. Five years ago, she might have walked, even skipped, as the girls across the way. Who had she been before the pain-filled weeks had brought her to Saint Anne's? And try as she did to recall her, that Theresa Freidmann remained a stranger.

As the morning wore on, she had company in the garden. An old man made his way along a gravel path, one leg dragging slowly up to parallel the other. She watched the toe of his slipper make a little furrow in the stones. Another walked by swiftly, head down and mumbling. Over on a wooden bench, there was an old woman with white adhesive tape wrapped around every finger on her hands. She sat, her fingers in her hair, rubbing, rubbing, rubbing. And in spite of the tape, great patches of her scalp showed bare.

Not many weeks before, Miss Freidmann would have been terrified by these patients, but her acquaintance and dominance over Maribel had given her a certain confidence. Still, she felt a revulsion. Was she, the child of Mama and Papa Freidmann, to spend her days in company such as this? She closed her eyes to Saint Anne's and at once her ears became tuned to the sounds.

They were the sounds of Canada recovering from a war. There was the sharp rap of a jack hammer, the rattle of garbage cans in a truck, the changing gears of the cars stopped at the intersection. Overhead, there were planes flying.

Oh, things had changed in five years. But then, so had she. Despite the lazy heat, she began to feel the challenge. When Herbert came, she would have another talk with him about the house. On that, she was quite determined. The house had to be put in order. It must be restored to the way it had been when Mama and Papa were alive. It was her one tie to a kindlier past. It had to go on the same.

Miss Freidmann was safely back upstairs and in bed when Mr. Dickey came. She was rested and alert, but as it happened, she didn't need to bring up the subject of the renters. He did.

"The man, Pete," he said, "is out of the army now and he wants to know if he can work on the roof in his spare time."

"Does he know how to shingle a roof?"

"I don't know. He says he's a handyman."

"I'll have to think about it. Do you know, Herbert," Miss Freidmann could contain her excitement no longer, "I was outside today?"

"Outside? How could you be outside?"

"In a wheelchair. I was out in the garden and I enjoyed it. I just hope it's warm tomorrow so I can go out again."

He covered his dismay. "You ought to be careful, Theresa. You might catch cold." And before long, he took his leave to walk morosely down the street to his apartment.

Whoever would have thought they'd get her up and outside in a wheelchair? Of course, that wouldn't detract from her sympathetic appeal as a politician's wife. It might even enhance it. Perhaps he might get his picture taken wheeling her in the garden. Only, a wife who could get about, even in a wheelchair, could be expected to meddle in all sorts of things. And Theresa was uncommonly shrewd.

He walked slowly, pondering. How was he ever going to

ask her to marry him? He felt an absolute fool just holding her hand. Once, he'd thought of trying to kiss her and when he had bent his head, she had said, "Herbert, what are you getting so close for?" His face reddened again as he remembered his discomfiture. Why couldn't he just ask her as though it was some sort of business arrangement? But then, he'd heard women weren't businesslike about marriage. Still, it wasn't as though either he or she . . . Oh, Good Lord. Never.

Yet, her money was practically a necessity. A Conservative was going to need some good strong backing the way the C.C.F. had swept the Province in the last election. And Theresa had the money. Actually, she just suited his needs to perfection. If only she would stay safe and sound, and out of the way, at Saint Anne's.

CHAPTER 14

Back at Saint Anne's, Miss Freidmann was having some thoughts of her own. She queried Emily Louise as to the abilities of the man, Pete. "Herbert says that man wants to shingle the roof. Do you think he can?"

"He might if the gin holds out. He wasn't much of a hand with my shoe, but the roof would be a bit bigger. He couldn't hardly miss."

"Well, anyway," Miss Freidmann said with satisfaction, "Herbert has got that girl out of the basement at last. I told him to get it filled up with coal."

"Coal?"

"Sacked coal."

"For shame. Have you no romance? Imagine some poor returning sailor going down in the dark of night to see Myrtle, and nothing to take in his arms but a sack of coal."

"Serve him right. Next time he would know enough to turn on the light before he went about taking people in his arms."

"It's much nicer in the dark. You ought to try it sometime. Of course, the dark of night isn't very romantic at Saint Anne's. All the old men wheezing and snoring. It's no use, Dearie, no matter how you look at it. There's no future here at all."

"Never mind the future. My mind is on the present just now. I've heard from Mr. Farraday. He's getting a start. He has some of the lots surveyed and the streets marked off. He's going to start pouring foundations for the first ten houses next week. You know, I think I was lucky to come across a man like Mr. Farraday. He seems to be a real business man. I wish I could say as much about Herbert. He's so vague about that man, Pete. How do I know if he can shingle a roof?"

"Do you want me to go and find out?"

"I don't like to keep asking you."

"It would be a pleasure. I took a bit of a fancy to Pete. Who knows, he might invite me up on the roof to help him hammer a nail or two."

"I'd be very grateful if you would go and see," Miss Freidmann said and admitted to herself her dependence on the girl. A dependence that seemed to be increasing day by day. She knew that Emily Louise gave of her time willingly, almost eagerly. She was a keen observer and her accounts, one could be sure, would be detailed and complete. "It's just that I'd like to know how things are going at the house . . ."

"I'll check up for you, Dearie. And I'll pay extra attention to the basement. You can count on me."

Emily Louise, to be truthful, rather enjoyed her errands for Miss Freidmann. They gave a purpose to the loose ends of her own life. It was amazing, she thought as she set out on the mission, how Miss Freidmann had blossomed. And underneath, Emily Louise suspected she wasn't shocked nearly as often as she pretended to be. And Emily Louise wasn't at all opposed to the prospect of another meeting with Annie and her husband, Pete.

Cool and trim on a summer day, she walked once again past the brick pillars at the gate. The house seemed strangely quiet. Summer, she thought, didn't help the place much.

Pete, stripped to the waist, lay on the uncut lawn on a khaki army blanket. The girl, Mary Ann, of all things, sat knitting. Emily Louise needed only one glance at Annie, sitting in a wicker chair, to know why. She was wearing white shorts and one of Pete's shirts hung full around her body. Her long hair hung in damp curls, but her stomach, distended and protruding, dominated her appearance. Without a doubt, Annie was pregnant.

They greeted Emily Louise with friendly curiosity. And they spoke with the candor of the farming communities which Emily Louise understood.

Pete said, "Hey, you come to tell us the landlady wants to raise the rent?"

Emily Louise laughed. "Nothing like that." She sat on the grass near them. "To be honest," she said, "the landlady wanted to be sure she was rid of Myrtle. She sent me out to find out how much you knew about shingling a roof. But, I'm sure she's really much more concerned about the basement than the roof."

"Hell, I can shingle anything.," Pete replied. "You can tell her so. It leaks the way it is, so what's she got to lose? And Myrtle's long gone, and a good thing, too. That dame was a stepper. A real stepper."

"Aw, Pete, she wasn't so bad," Annie put in. "I kind of miss her."

"Well, I don't," Pete said abruptly. "All night, tee-heeing and hee-hawing down there. Never knew who she had or how many."

"One night," Mary Ann said wisely, "there was a soldier and a sailor."

"Mary Ann," Annie said sharply, "you go in the house and find us a nice cold beer."

The girl got to her feet lightly, indolently. "Mama's pregnant," she explained. "We have to humor her. She gets cravings."

"Jeez," Pete said when she had gone. "That kid's smart, Annie. Too damn smart. Knows too much."

"It's your fault, Pete," Annie said amiably. "You're too noisy. She stays awake nights. I keep telling you to be quiet."

"Quiet? Jeez, woman, I've been a long time in the army. How can you expect a man to be quiet?" He said to Emily Louise, "She's mad because she's pregnant."

"I'm not mad, you big ape," Annie defended. "Anyway, it's your fault." She explained to Emily Louise, "Every New Year, he gets crazy drunk."

"I wasn't drunk."

"You were, too. You were drunk and you weren't careful."

"Kee-rist! I've told you a hundred times, I was careful. It's those damn army supplies. Never could trust anything you got in the army."

"Well, I don't care," Annie said. "I like babies. Only, you can tell that landlady," she addressed Emily Louise, "that we aren't leaving until it's born. I'm not having a baby up there in the backwoods. I want a doctor and a hospital."

"Under the circumstances," Emily Louise said quickly, "I'm sure she'll understand."

"Well, that fool of a lawyer she has doesn't understand," Pete said plaintively. "Always coming around, 'When will the house be vacant?' he asks. Don't he know it takes nine months to have a baby?"

"I don't think he has much experience," Emily Louise murmured. "About babies and things like that."

Pete said morosely, "You never can tell. Look at Lester. Puny little flea. Couldn't hardly lift an army pack sack. But they had four kids quicker than it took her to get to bed at night. And now, he's out of the army and going to college this fall. I bet she has another by spring."

"Dorothy doesn't care," Annie defended. "She has an apartment. She's comfortable . . ."

"Apartment? Two rooms and a community kitchen and upstairs in your night shirt to use the W.C. 'And my Lester,' she says, all hoity-toity, 'is going to be an engineer.'"

"Dorothy is ambitious," Annie said. "They'll make out. You wait and see."

"They'll make out," Pete agreed. "And that's fine. Just so long as they ain't making out over my bedroom ceiling."

"Have they left?" Emily Louise asked.

"They left all right," Pete said. "Last week. That should make the landlady happy."

And Emily Louise knew that in that respect at least, Miss Freidmann would be happy. She took her leave before she was tempted to partake of the beer the child, Mary Ann, was bringing. Liquor on her breath would never do at Saint Anne's.

Gaily, she relayed her information to Miss Freidmann. "Well, I met your renters again and you won't be rid of them for awhile. Annie's pregnant."

Miss Freidmann said aghast, "Not the other one, too?"

"The other one it is," Emily Louise said cheerily. "Dorothy and all of hers are gone. Her Lester is going to college. But, Annie won't move up north until her baby is born."

"When is that?"

Emily Louise considered. "It should be in a month or two. Probably about the end of September. She got caught at New Year."

"Good Heavens, girl. You don't have to find out things so thoroughly." She hesitated. "How do you know she got . . . how do you know it was New Year?"

"Pete told me. Annie said he was drunk and Pete insisted he wasn't, only that . . ." Emily Louise giggled, "the army supplies weren't any good."

Miss Freidmann considered the information in silence and Emily Louise added an explanation. "You know the army is very understanding. When they give a man a forty-eight hour pass, they give him the necessary precautions. Temptation being what it is and all. Besides, just in case they're not too discriminating, it's cheaper than medical care."

"It's immoral."

"It certainly is. Only the married men would dream of taking them, so it keeps the married ones protected and leaves the rest of us sinners."

"It didn't help Pete."

"Not if you believe his story. But, never mind, Dearie. The baby will soon be born and they'll all go north and you will have your house all safe and sound."

"I'll have the house and it may be safe. I'm not so sure about it being sound. It will probably never be the same again."

"That it won't, my Pretty," Emily Louise agreed and added quietly, "It's the war and all that. None of us, people or houses, will likely ever be the same again. There's bound to be a few scuffs and scars somewhere."

Alone again, Miss Freidmann pondered the parting

words. She had been sheltered from the war and yet she was scuffed and scarred more than most. Worse even than the soldiers. Doctor Myers kept telling her that. Still, her scuffs were like those on her house. They showed up, but perhaps they weren't the worst kind. It occurred to her that the scuffs--the ones like Emily Louise had that didn't show at all--perhaps they hurt the worst.

Miss Freidmann was interrupted from her reveries as Emily Louise burst back into the room. She spoke, her voice tragic, "Mister Fred's gone."

"Gone? Run away?"

"Dead."

"Dead? Did you just find him dead?"

"No, thank the Saints for that. Bob found him this afternoon. He just lay dead in his bed. Just imagine, poor old George, right in there with him and not able to say a word. Only lay there watching him and waiting for someone to come."

"How do you know he watched him? Maybe he just died quietly while George was asleep and he never noticed."

"You don't have to see Death, Dearie. Awake or asleep, you feel it. It's all through the room. You only need to walk past someone who's dead and you know it. I don't know why, but you do."

"What happened?" Miss Freidmann asked, not knowing how to escape asking. "Did he have a heart attack?"

"No, another stroke. Bob said his face was all twisted and red. Oh, Dear Mother. Poor old Mister Fred. And Bob said he was laughing at a good one only this morning. I wonder how George will manage without him."

"Move him in with someone else. Someone who can talk."

"That would only make him feel worse. Mister Fred and George talked with their eyes. They understood one another. I don't know how I'll ever face George while I scrub that bed."

"Have they taken him away?"

"Oh, he's gone, taken away and everything. It's a

shame, so it is. I wish now I'd given him an extra spoonful of sugar on his porridge this morning."

"Why?"

"Oh, I don't know. Sweeten the way, I guess. He wasn't a Catholic and there doesn't seem to be anyone to pray for him. I think I'll go to the chapel myself tonight and say a little prayer or two."

"Lots of people die without prayers, I suppose."

"That's their own look out. Old Mister Fred couldn't be saying his for himself."

Miss Freidmann looked closely at Emily Louise. There was an almost reverent sadness upon her open face. "I can't understand you at all. I mean, why are you so upset? Only the other morning you were grumbling about having to feed him."

"I grumble about you, too, my Pretty. But, I shouldn't want to walk in and find you all glassy eyed and dead with no warning at all."

"I'll try," Miss Freidmann said dryly, "to get seriously ill and die gradually, so you'll be prepared."

"It's yourself you ought to be worrying about preparing. Have you decided to die a Catholic or a Jew?"

"Neither."

"Why?"

"I couldn't be a Catholic. I'd get all mixed up with the beads. And it wouldn't be fair to Mama to become a Jew. Anyway, I'm not planning on dying yet."

"Well, don't leave it until the last minute. Around Saint Anne's, people seem to die without any planning." And leaving Miss Freidmann to speculate on her inevitable fate as neither Catholic nor Jew nor anything else, Emily Louise reluctantly took a basin of hot water heavily laced with disinfectant and made her way to room Eight. Sister Mary Phillipe, her sleeves rolled to the elbows, came bustling in to supervise. She opened the windows wide and began to empty the drawer of the bedside table.

Sister Mary Phillipe fought grime, dust, and untidiness in exactly the same way that Sister Mary Sophia fought pain, suffering, and death. And on the road to Heaven, Emily Louise decided, there was as much a need for the Mary Phillipes to keep the way bright and shining as there was for the Mary Sophias to extend a comforting hand.

Mary Phillipe was completely engrossed in the bedside table. She found a can, half filled with tobacco, and a bent and blackened pipe. She put them together in a paper sack. She reached back in the drawer and found a pocket knife and it rattled against the can when she dropped it, too, into the sack.

Emily Louise stripped the bed and began to wash the white metal. George, she knew, watched every movement of her hands. And George heard the scraping of the urinal as Sister Mary Phillipe took it from the stand and put it with the wash basin and the bed pan to be sterilized. And George saw her take Mister Fred's glasses and put them in the sack with the tobacco and the pipe and the knife. Emily Louise concentrated on her cleaning. The belongings of the dead, at least the dead of Saint Anne's, were so pitifully few.

"The only time," Sister Mary Phillipe was saying briskly, "that these tables ever get properly cleaned is in between patients. How long was he here?"

"I'm not sure. Years." Emily Louise barely whispered the words. She could feel George's speechless gaze turned toward her.

They worked quickly and quietly. They turned the mattress, put on a new rubber sheet, and stretched the stiff, clean linens tautly across the bed. Emily Louise put the cases on the pillows, pleating them neatly. Sister Mary Phillipe went over and closed the windows. She turned, sniffed, and opened one wide again. "There's still a strange odor in here," she observed. "I can't understand it. We've cleaned it well. I think it needs a bit more fresh air."

Emily Louise nodded, "I'll come back in and close it after awhile," she said. And when Sister Mary Phillipe had left, she went down the hall until she found Bob. "Be an angel, Bob," she said, " and go and tend to George."

"What's wrong with George?"

"We were in there cleaning," she began, and afterwards Bob was never quite sure if it was a sob or just the soft lilt that made her voice so husky as she stood near to him in the dimly lighted hallway. "We were in there cleaning," she continued, "and the poor old darlin' went and messed in his bed."

CHAPTER 15

All through the summer, Miss Freidmann spent her afternoons, and frequently part of her mornings as well, propped in her wheelchair in the garden. Sometimes, Herbert Dickey came to sit with her, nervous and ill at ease on the edge of a green slatted garden bench. Always, his eyes strayed beyond Miss Freidmann to keep a careful watch on one or another of the patients who crept in an unsteady parade along the pathways.

Only one feature of the garden endeared itself to Herbert Dickey. Maribel was never allowed there. The garden gate and picket fence, so the story was told, were never designed to confine Maribel. On the single occasion she had been allowed outside, she had promptly disappeared. No one knew what wild call she heard and answered, only that Maribel took to her heels and fairly flew, to vanish among the streets and alleys of Saskatoon. And when, at last, they called the Mounties, Maribel was still flitting here, there, and everywhere. Now downtown, now by the river, now in the city parks, until at last a trainman found her down at the Canadian Pacific Railway depot, contentedly sharing a boxcar with some of Canada's knights of the open road. Somehow, Maribel emerged unscathed from her escapade which, Emily Louise insisted, was certainly a blessing because it would have taken a bit of explaining on the records.

Mr. Farraday also came to visit occasionally in the garden. In spite of the name, Miss Freidmann was inclined to suspect that Mr. Farraday was a Jew and she never regretted the impulse that had caused her to embark in business with him. Mr. Farraday had an eye for detail and a mind for finance. He had a family of sons and daughters who "were going to amount to something" if he had to build houses all over Saskatchewan to educate them. And those houses, she was quite positive, would all be built and sold at a profit.

So, as the summer progressed, Miss Freidmann came to enjoy her days in the garden. She bought an air cushion to ease the pressure of the hours of sitting and she sat and read and contemplated. Occasionally, she fretted over her legs and her knees which would probably never, Doctor Myers had confided, get much straighter than they were. Sometimes, she sat watching the limping, limited movements of her companions in the garden with envy. Then, hearing their incoherent and feeble muttering, she settled for lame limbs and a sound mind. She watched a patient on crutches, wondering if she would ever walk in such a manner, but a glance at her thin arms and twisted wrists and she knew she never would.

There was only one hope for Theresa Freidmann. She learned this through the long days of summer. She had to use her mind and her head to keep enough money on hand so she would never lack for someone to push her about in the wheelchair. Money alone could make bearable a stark existence at Saint Anne's. So, she sat through the summer sun and heat, until Emily Louise told her casually one day, she should be ripe like the wheat in the fields on the prairie.

And for her own part, even while talking lightly, Emily Louise felt a dreadful loneliness, a loneliness of completion and ending coming in on the winds that stirred the golden grain. The same gold stole into the city. It was in the haze of the sky, in the weeds darkening the cracks of the sidewalks, and in the dry heads of wild grass growing on a vacant lot across the street.

And while Miss Freidmann sat in the wheelchair with the sun's rays warm on her throbbing joints, Emily Louise, in the annex one day, shrugged from the starched stiffness of her hospital smock. She found a bright, flowered skirt and a blouse of pale green and she gazed long enough in the mirror to approve of the way her hair fell in russet curls about her shoulders. Irish O'Shaughnessy had been disposed to run his fingers, twisting and caressing, through her hair. And her thoughts of Irish O'Shaughnessy, the infinite joy in the touch of his fingers, caused her to close her gray-green eyes, unwilling to recognize the emotion she knew to be there. She left Saint Anne's to walk up the street to the florist.

She came out with an armful of flowers, gay flowers, bachelor buttons, pink snapdragons, and daisies. She waited at the corner for a street car, boarded it, and rode until she came to what she had taken to referring to as Miss Freidmann's cemetery.

She went past the black wrought iron gates and soon her feet left the gravel path. She trod, with a sense of familiarity, over dry, curling prairie grass while the grasshoppers whirred into the air before her. And every drumming wing-beat stirred the hurt that lay high in her throat.

She made her way directly to one corner of the cemetery and once there, she dropped down to her knees. Her exploring fingers found a sunken can. She filled it with water and arranged a few of the blossoms. From grave to tiny grave, she went. Once, her fingers came upon a concrete lamb hidden beneath the branches of a dry and withered rose. Once, she brushed the dust from an angel which hovered, wings outspread, above a stone. Emily Louise had first come upon the tiny graves when she had come searching for the name of Freidmann. She had come upon them and hurried on. Now, she came to linger and to love.

She read the names and sighed a little over the dates that were carved into the stones. And when the flowers had all been placed, Emily Louise sat among them on the grass in the dry, stifling heat. Each baby, she wanted to pluck from the ground and hold to her and love. Each baby, alone under the hard earth, had somehow become the unborn child of herself and Irish O'Shaughnessy. Jealously, she lay back and clutched them to her heart. It was early in the autumn of 1945 and that morning Mother Superior had given her a check. "Your debt, Emily Louise," she said, "is paid. It is paid in full. You may stay on at Saint Anne's or you may go on to other things. May the Blessed Mother guide you, my child."

So, Emily Louise had bought the flowers. And here, here with the little lost ones, she knew there was a part of the debt that would never be paid. She'd had the love and she'd lost. The loss had to be greater for the knowing. And there, where Death had become as poignant a thing as an unborn child, she closed her eyes and called him back to her. "Irish O'Shaughnessy," she complained, "do you know how lonely a girl can feel for the touch of a man's hand?"

He only teased from the distance. "And having known the touch of Irish O'Shaughnessy, my Sweet, it will be very hard to be content with the touch of another. Perhaps, some time . . ."

"No," she whispered it into the day. "Don't let me go." The warm wind in her hair became the caress of a lover. "Our baby," she whispered, "must have been the sweetest of them all." The hard earth could have been only the strength of his shoulder beneath her head. Almost, she could feel again his arm about her, the touch of his fingers, warm upon her body.

Her reverie was broken by the coarse crunch of car wheels on gravel. Startled, she jumped to her feet. "This, my girl," she chided herself, "is no place for your day-dreams. When next you wake, you'll be finding yourself chief mourner at a funeral."

However, it was no funeral procession moving into the cemetery, but it was a hearse. It came slowly, long, sleek, and shining in the afternoon sun and it stopped in front of the office near the gate. The driver, stepping out, looked long and curiously at Emily Louise as she stood uncertainly among the graves. Composing herself, she left the grass and walked toward him along the path.

As she came closer, he nodded, smiled uncertainly, then meeting Emily Louise's friendly gaze, he said with obvious satisfaction, "Isn't she a beaut?"

"I beg your pardon?"

"The hearse. Isn't she a beaut?" He ran the back of his hand lovingly over the smooth paint.

"It looks very nice," Emily Louise agreed. "Although, I'm not exactly an authority on hearses, you understand."

"Well, this is a good one. Have a look." He opened the wide doors at the back and exposed the black upholstery and the metal fittings. "Look at that," he said. "Isn't that pretty fancy? You know, things have come a long, long way. When I was a kid on the prairie, my old man used to haul the coffins on the back of the truck from the livery yard. Got to be a bit more fancy nowadays, otherwise you'd go out of business. People want a funeral with class." He shook his head, ruefully. "The better the coffin, the better the corpse. And a shiny new hearse adds a lot to a funeral."

"Is it new?" Emily Louise asked, finding it hard to share his enthusiasm for the conveyance.

"Just got her today," he acknowledged. "Guess this means the end of old Carrie, there. Funny, she looked pretty good right up until I drove the new one alongside. Kind of hate to let her go, she never once broke down in a funeral procession. Got quite attached to her. Still, I guess she'll fetch a good price. Used cars are high."

"That's not exactly a car," Emily Louise speculated, rather enjoying this cheerful stranger. "Who would want to buy a used hearse?"

"Plenty," he smiled. "Paint her up and take out the stretchers, and you've got a nice little delivery truck. Why, you can't buy a delivery truck nowadays. Know how long I've had my order in for this baby? Three years. Imagine that. Three whole years. Don't worry, there will be plenty of takers for old Carrie."

Emily Louise became suddenly thoughtful. "A delivery truck?" she mused. "You know, I've just had an idea about your hearse, only I prefer the word 'truck,' if it's all the same to you. I think I know just the person who needs it. How much is it worth?"

"About eight hundred and fifty dollars, I figure."

"Isn't that a lot of money?"

"Like I told you, used cars are high."

"Could it be painted a different color and have all those . . . those rods taken off the sides."

"Oh, I can get the rods taken off, but it costs quite a bit to get a car painted."

"The lady I was thinking of who might buy it, doesn't have much money."

"Neither does the man who's selling it. This burying business isn't all roses, you know. Competition and all that. Eight seventy-five, all painted and ready to go."

"I'll run right back and ask her. Will you wait and not sell it until you hear from me?"

"Reckon I can wait a day or two."

"I'll let you know right away."

Back at Saint Anne's, Emily Louise, green blouse, flowered skirt, and all, ran up the stairs to Room Two. Miss Freidmann looked surprised and pleased to see her. "You look pretty," she volunteered. "Much prettier than in white."

"Bless you, Dearie, but we've no time for compliments. I've just practically haggled my way into buying you a car."

"A car? You're mad."

"I'm not mad. A car is just what you need. You could get out and see your house."

"I couldn't even sit in a car."

"You could in this one. It's a little truck affair. You can have your chair wheeled right inside."

"And then what? I say 'giddyap' and it goes?"

"I'll drive you. I used to drive my daddy's truck."

"I'll have to think about it."

"You'll have to think fast. I told him I'd let him know right away. And he won't be keeping it long, used cars are hard to get."

"How much?"

"Eight hundred and seventy-five dollars."

Miss Freidmann gasped. "Eight hundred and seventy five dollars. I could be carried piggy-back for that."

"Perhaps, but in a car, you can go all sorts of places. Why," Emily Louise promised rashly, "I'd take you out for a drive every time I had a day off. You need a car. And as scarce as they are, this one is a real bargain. You'll never miss the money."

"I wish you wouldn't rush me into things like this. I like to have more time to think and I don't know anything about cars. Perhaps, I ought to ask Herbert."

"Herbert?" Emily Louise tried to hide her dismay. "Herbert? He's a lawyer, not a car dealer. And you know you always say he doesn't understand your business deals. Anyway, you have to make up your mind tonight. I told the man I'd call him right back. If you buy it, I'll drive you out to see your house just as soon as Doctor Myers will let you go."

"How will you get me in and out of it?"

"It's a little truck affair, like I told you. And it has big, wide doors at the back so you can go right in, chair and all."

"I've never seen a car like that."

"That's just what I mean. It's the chance of a lifetime."

Miss Freidmann sat, considering. Belying the furrows across her brow, her eyes were bright and a little smile lifted the corners of her lips. "Herbert can't abide my sudden decisions," she said. "Poor Herbert. He can't possibly realize what it would mean to me to see that house. You tell the man I will buy his truck, or whatever it is. And it had better be a good one."

Emily Louise felt a few misgivings as she went down to telephone. Eight hundred and seventy-five dollars was a lot of money. Still, she thought, that car was going to do Miss Freidmann a lot more good than buying all those weedy vacant lots. And anyway, the venture with Mr. Farraday should pay dividends before too long. She telephoned her acquaintance of the afternoon and assured him that a check would be waiting just as soon as the car was stripped of its trimmings and delivered to the door of Saint Anne's. And when he asked what color he should have it painted, Emily Louise almost sang her reply into the telephone. "Kelly green," she replied. A nice, bright, Kelly green."

Mr. Dickey, when he was told the news, reacted exactly as Miss Freidmann had expected he would. He lectured her, from his wide professional experience, on the folly of snap decisions. He was skeptical as to the condition of any automobile sold sight unseen. And when Miss Freidmann took it upon herself to remind him that Emily Louise had seen the car, he only shook his head glumly and asked if Miss Freidmann was sure that young woman had a driver's license. Somehow, though, it seemed not to occur to him to question Emily Louise's explanation for the delay in the delivery of the car.

"It's at the garage," she stated. "They are making a little metal ramp to fit on the back so it will be easy to wheel your chair right in." She did not add that after one glimpse into the gloomy, dark interior of the vehicle, she had ordered the partition removed between the front and the back. Nor that this meant a considerably longer delay because she had to arrange for the payment of that herself.

When the car was at last delivered to the door of Saint Anne's, Mr. Dickey seemed almost eager to accept Miss Freidmann's invitation to accompany them on the visit to her house the following Sunday. And even Emily Louise approved of the arrangement. "He will be handy," she said, "to steady your chair until we get into the swing of things."

Doctor Myers, too, had nothing but encouragement for the venture. "At last," he said, "you are taking a step forward, at last." And with unusual pampering, he suggested that Miss Freidmann be given a couple of aspirin tablets before she left so the afternoon would not be marred by pain.

On the morning of the visit, Emily Louise instructed Miss Freidmann to lie quietly and conserve her strength. "I know you've been up a lot, Dearie. But the ride and all is apt to tire you out."

Miss Freidmann tried to comply. Nevertheless, by the time Emily Louise came in the afternoon to dress her, she was in a fever of excitement. She felt anticipation, as though the sight of the familiar house would erase the reality of crippled limbs and the long years at Saint Anne's. She allowed herself to be fitted out in her most pointed uplifts, the pinkest nightgown, and the robe.

"You need a dress," Emily Louise observed. "Your nightgown will probably be caught in the breeze and *whoosh*. But I'll be careful and tuck the robe well around."

"Tuck a blanket," Miss Freidmann ordered. "That robe will whoosh just as quickly as the gown."

Miss Freidmann was lifted into her chair and taken downstairs onto the sidewalk. She felt the curious glances of passersby and was glad that Emily Louise had wrapped the woolen shawl about her shoulders. The pink of the robe was softened by the lacy layers of wool. For only a moment, she worried about her appearance because almost immediately her attention was taken by the green vehicle parked brazenly in the "Emergency Only" space by the door. "Is that *it*?" she asked.

"That's it, Dearie. Isn't it a beauty? I told you it was."

"It looks a little funny," Miss Freidmann began.

"Here we are." Emily Louise swiftly wheeled the chair to the rear of the vehicle. "Here's the little ramp. The man made it specially for your chair. Tricky, isn't it?"

"Where's Herbert? I thought he was going to hold my chair." Panic and alarm trembled in Miss Freidmann's voice as the chair tilted on its way up the ramp and then rolled toward the front of the conveyance.

"He's coming. He just turned the corner. I'll have him all cooped up in here with you in just a minute." And Mr. Dickey, arriving late, had little more than time for one quick appraisal of the vehicle before his head bent close to Miss Freidmann's and the door tightly closed behind him.

With a gay little wave to Bob who grinned from a second

floor window, Emily Louise edged slowly into the traffic. A smile lurked behind the gray-green eyes and began to pull at the corners of her lips. One more glimpse of Bob's face and she would have burst into uncontrollable laughter. He, too, had noticed Herbert Dickey's hesitation. And while Miss Freidmann rode, perhaps, uncomfortably, she was blissfully unaware. Crowded in beside her, Herbert Dickey knew only too well that he was trundling down the streets of Saskatoon in a Kelly green hearse.

CHAPTER 17

It was not until the following March that Miss Freidmann left Saint Anne's and went home. During those weeks, a transformation had been worked in the house. The walls had been painted, the paneling re-stained. Emily Louise had, on one memorable occasion, taken Miss Freidmann, wheelchair and all, to a downtown store where she selected new kitchen linoleum and a thick new carpet for the parlor. The piano had been sent out for refinishing and when it was returned, the last whiskey stains had disappeared. It had all cost a lot of money and Herbert Dickey had voiced his misgivings.

"All that money, Theresa? Just for painting and varnishing?"

"My stocks paid good dividends last year. You said so yourself."

"But why did you get such an expensive carpet?"

And then there had been his shock at her reply, "If I don't get a good one, it won't stand up to the wear and tear of this wheelchair."

"I don't understand."

"I'm going home to live."

"You can't possibly live at home, Theresa."

"Doctor Myers says I can."

"But, how will you manage without the hospital and all the pills and things?" He seized the opportunity, "Theresa, you need someone to look after you."

"I've thought of that. I've asked Emily Louise."

"What?"

"I've asked Emily Louise. I think she will be perfect. Cheerful and lively. Resourceful, too . . . if only she doesn't go running off and getting married . . ."

"Theresa," Mr. Dickey realized with sudden clarity that he had let things drift too long. "What's wrong with getting married?"

"Why, nothing, Herbert," Miss Freidmann replied with innocence. "Only I'm used to her and I shouldn't like to have to keep changing companions."

"She seems quite attracted to men," Mr. Dickey ventured. "She's lively and . . . and all that sort of thing. I shouldn't be at all surprised if she wanted to marry."

"Then I'll keep raising her wages so she can't afford to leave, or else build her a cottage next door. I've taken quite a fancy to Emily Louise."

Who would have thought she would take it into her head to go home? Mr. Dickey felt desperate. Obviously, he had to speak up now. If she ever got outside of Saint Anne's, there was no telling how she would spend her money. "Two women," he said, "alone in that big house. You need a man around."

"Emily Louise has taken care of that."

"Oh?"

"Bob's coming every week on his day off to do the odd jobs. Bob's a great comfort. And Emily Louise can drive so well, we might even travel somewhere later on. You know, Herbert," Miss Freidmann said wistfully, "I've never really been anywhere."

"Theresa," he spoke quickly, his visions of a well-financed political career ending up in Europe or Timbuktu or Heaven knew where. "Why don't you marry me?" There, he'd said it and it hadn't been so bad. He began to feel better, more self-assured. Theresa was practical. She'd know there wouldn't be many chances and he was sure she wouldn't expect he would live with her as a husband was supposed to live with a wife. Not many women were as realistic as Theresa.

"Marry you?"

"Marry me," he repeated more firmly. He hadn't expected her to be so startled. Surely, she must have suspected he had some reason for coming to see her all this time. "You need someone to look after you."

"I certainly do," she agreed. "I need a woman. Herbert, have you any idea how I have to be looked after?"

He hesitated. He hadn't really thought of how she had to be looked after. She was very crippled. Yes, there would be all sorts of little things, his mind refused to consider them. "We could have a maid."

"No," Miss Freidmann shook her head. "I'm afraid that would never do at all. I couldn't marry you, Herbert. Or anyone at all. But, I'm glad you asked me. You know, I've always rather hoped that someone would ask me sometime. And I do enjoy your company. You'll have to come to the house and see us, but be sure to come when Emily Louise is in a good mood. She doesn't always approve of you."

"Why?" he asked glumly and wondered why, lying bent and crippled like that, she'd say "No" to a proposal. You'd think she'd jump at the chance.

"She thinks you're after my fortune. Never mind, Herbert. It's not much of a fortune. If I'm not careful, I'll end up spending it all myself. Anyway, I'll still need you to look after my legal affairs."

"I'm thinking of going into politics," he ventured. "I'd like to run for Parliament."

"In Ottawa?"

He nodded, she might still be persuaded to help. "Of course, I'll probably have to start on the Provincial, or even the local level, first. Of course, the C.C.F. is pretty strong now, but nationally, it's time for a swing to the Conservatives, don't you think?"

"Good Heavens, Herbert. I don't know a thing about politics. Never mind, I'll vote for you anyway. And perhaps Emily Louise will, too."

"The trouble is, it takes a lot of money. Travelling, making speeches, and all that."

"Everything takes money. You can't do anything without it. You ought to be investing, Herbert. I can't think why you don't try real estate." Miss Freidmann looked at him kindly as he picked up his hat, preparing to leave. He had, after all, devoted many hours to her cause and frankly, she admitted to herself, she hoped he would devote more.

It was gratifying, having a gentleman come to call. "I think you'll make a very good politician," she said.

He nodded.

"And thanks for asking me, Herbert. I won't mind so much, being an old maid, now that I've been asked."

After he had gone, Miss Freidmann, unable to resist sharing her moment of triumph, confided to Emily Louise. "He proposed."

"Proposed what?"

• "Marriage, of course."

"Old Dickey Boy? Well, bless his heart. I thought he'd never get up the courage. Are you going to?"

"Of course not. You know I could never get married."

"Why?"

"Oh, goodness, girl. You've told me yourself," Miss Freidmann flushed, "I'm in no shape for it."

Emily Louise's eyes wrinkled with amusement. "Maybe he's still young enough to bend a little."

"You're shameless."

"I know. I'm a sinner. I just can't seem to help thinking of such things. Irish O'Shaughnessy was a beautiful lover."

"If I have you for a companion, I suppose you will be running off and getting married. I realize I have no right to ask you not to. But I'll pay you well."

"If I do, I'll marry Bob. And we'll share him. To be truthful, the idea of being your companion rather appeals to me. I can hardly wait to take you around and show you the wicked world."

Looking down, Miss Freidmann saw the hump in the bed over her bent knees. She saw her wrists and fingers, warped and twisted askew, and she saw her bosom pointed forward, straight and firm. The years at Saint Anne's had been many and long. "You must admit," she said thoughtfully, "I deserve it. I've been in the saintly one for a long, long time."

As the time neared when they would leave, Emily Louise

became plainly sentimental. "For a year," she mourned, "I've been wanting to leave this place and now it brings tears to my eyes to say goodbye. Do you know what they're going to do to George? Those doctors up at the University have got their eyes on him and they're going to have another go at his head. And there he is, poor speechless soul, looking at his wife and the wee girl on the table right beside him and thinking he'll be walking around and talking when they're done. It's thankful I am that I'll not be here when they come to take him away."

And on another occasion, she questioned bleakly, "What about Maribel? Don't you think she'll miss us?"

"She'll miss the mints," Miss Freidmann remarked dryly.

"Perhaps, we can drop by every now and then and bring her some. Oh well, the old world keeps spinning and it's not for the likes of us to be holding it up. Your duds are all packed and we'll soon be on our way."

Miss Freidmann said, a sudden nervousness overwhelming her, "I hope I'll be all right. I have my pills if I can't sleep and you will be there. Only I've been here so long. Do you think the house will seem empty and lonely?"

"Not a bit. We have the radio. And then there's Peter."

"Who's Peter?"

"I've spoken for a terrier puppy. We have to have a dog. Besides," and the roguish light was back in Emily Louise's eyes, "I'll never miss Saint Anne's as long as I can go around mopping up after Peter."

So, the day of departure came. Miss Freidmann was dressed and settled in her very own wheelchair and then taken downstairs to wait impatiently in the reception room of Saint Anne's. Emily Louise had gone to get her suitcase from her tiny room in the annex and, predictably, she lingered, finding it hard to say her final farewell.

She wrinkled her nose as she picked up her old black suitcase. She had taken the precaution of spraying all her clothes before she packed. However, bedbugs or not, she gazed about the little room with fondness. Here, she had felt the first pangs of her love for Irish O'Shaughnessy. The room knew all her longings and her tears. Here, he had been summoned from the mists to caress her. And here, he had marvelled with her at the beauty of the child who lived, as the Blessed Mother had told her, in some beautiful home of love. So, Emily Louise tip-toed from the room and closed the door with reverence. The tiny chamber, she would remember as an intimate sacristy to Love.

She joined Miss Freidmann in the reception room and, together, they bade their goodbyes to the Sisters and to Bob, who put the suitcases in the car. Then, they were out on the sidewalk and the brick walls of Saint Anne's stood staunch and solid behind them.

"Chest out," Emily Louise said brightly. "I'll soon have you up in your cage."

"Like a monkey," Miss Freidmann said as, inside the vehicle, Emily Louise secured the chair with blocks. "Well, I suppose I'm lucky. It always seemed to me that most of the patients leave Saint Anne's in a hearse."

"That they do, my Pretty." Emily Louise fought the temptation to tell. "This is our moment of victory. We ought to be flying some sort of flag, like a bedpan on a white sheet." She pulled out into the traffic.

"Or a nightshirt," Miss Freidmann suggested. "A night shirt is the real badge of Saint Anne's. You know, I think I first began to improve when I got out of those nightshirts and into a nightgown again."

"You should have married your old Dickey, you know."
"Why?"

"Well, if putting on a nightgown will unbend you, just think what having one taken off would do."

And despite her crippled limbs, Miss Freidmann felt an odd surge of anticipation creep over her as Emily Louise drove smoothly along the streets of Saskatoon, remarking casually, "We've come a long way, my Pretty. But, take it from me. There's all sorts of little things ahead. All sorts of things."

EPILOGUE

Back at Saint Anne's, Sister Mary Sophia stood with her hand still upon the door. She had said goodbye to Miss Freidmann and wished her well. And she had extracted a promise from Emily Louise to come back to the little chapel now and then for Mass.

"Indeed I will, Sister." The soft, deep warmth of the voice still lingered in her ears.

Their car had disappeared down the street. Still, Sister Mary Sophia lingered by the door. "Saint Anne's Home For The Chronically Ill And The Aged." The golden letters were a promise etched upon the door.

When she had first come to Saint Anne's, she had thought, in her ignorance, that all life ended here. It didn't, of course. That much, at least, had been taught her in a way she had never quite understood before. Life never ended. Sometimes it had to change and then go on.

Sister Mary Sophia acknowledged that she was going to miss Emily Louise. There had been a vitality to the girl. A glimpse of life that Sister Mary Sophia had never known. A life that she felt no regrets for not knowing. And yet, Emily Louise added to life. She gave it a perspective. She remembered Emily Louise coming to her that morning to say goodbye.

"Thank you, Sister," she said. "Thank you for laying your dear hands on my little one and blessing him." How had she known?

"He was so precious, Sister. Dark and beautiful, like an O'Shaughnessy should be. It's only right you should be the one to bless him. And now he lives with love."

Sister Mary Sophia trembled. Perhaps the anesthetic had not been deep enough. Had there been a fleeting moment of consciousness? "You promised," she said gently, "never to ask."

"And it's not forgetting I am, Sister. Or asking either. It

was the Blessed Mother herself who told me when I prayed, that where he went, there love would be with him."

"Perfect love," Sister Mary Sophia sighed softly. "The love of a little child."

Sister Mary Sophia looked again up the street. Then she closed the door of Saint Anne's with a little click and turned away.

Emily Louise had been right. So tragically right. The child had, indeed, been born exactly as she described, dark-haired, sweet, and beautiful. And she had placed her hands upon him in blessing. She had baptized him, she remembered, very swiftly, hoping as she held him that the tiny body would respond in the way of the newborn to life. She had waited and prayed in vain. Truly, the child did, as Emily Louise insisted, dwell with love. He would always be even more perfect and beautiful than in her dreams.

Sister Mary Sophia sighed as she turned and made her way upstairs. There would be other girls coming. But until one came, there would be extra work to do.

In Room Two, Sister Mary Phillipe was already busily cleaning. The bed had been stripped and washed. Clean linens, in a neat little pile, waited on the bedside table. A girl in blue was washing window sills and woodwork. Sister Mary Phillipe paused only briefly in her work to comment, "I can't understand, Mary Sophia, what Superior was thinking of to let that poor woman go away, as crippled and helpless as she was. I don't know how she's ever going to manage."

Sister Mary Sophia neatly folded a newspaper to line the dresser drawers, knowing exactly where the fold should go to make it fit. "You needn't worry about that, Mary Phillipe," she said and was surprised at the lightness of her own voice. "Miss Freidmann is going to be quite all right. She has Emily Louise."

ABOUT THE AUTHOR

Joan Darlington Beam, my first wife, was born October 20, 1919, in Essex, England. Her father was a farmer of considerable means. Joan's memories of England included a huge, rambling farm house with many chimneys and hours spent gathering heather and other wildflowers from the surrounding green fields.

But the family seemed to be plagued by bad luck. Mr. Darlington suffered a serious injury requiring a long recovery period when he was kicked by a cow. This, combined with the accidental destruction of some farm equipment and the loss of almost all their cattle due to disease, forced the family to auction what was left of the farm and immigrate to Canada.

The train trip across Canada to the province of Alberta was long. It seemed to everyone that Canada was a world all its own. There was nothing but land in every direction with no apparent end to it.

The Darlingtons' destination was Lougheed, a small town in eastern Alberta. It was located on the open prairie and consisted of a few stores and grain elevators. The entire area was bleak and uninviting— open spaces for miles and little protection from the arctic winds.

The final lap of their journey took them only a few more miles, but seemed to go on forever. Rounding a curve in the road, they reached the isolated farm house that was to be home for the next few years. The structure was old, unpainted, and not built for the cold Alberta winters. By this time, the family's finances were poor, but there was enough to pay the rent and get the farm work started. The situation seemed desperate, but this was only the beginning of much hardship that was to follow.

The first year yielded a good crop of wheat, but this sold for only 17 cents per bushel. The following years brought the Great Depression and only more disasters. Drought, hail, and grasshoppers meant hard times for everyone. Their only income was the $20 per month paid by the local school teacher for room and board. Joan learned to hate the prairie with its long, cold winters.

Better times did not come until after World War II began. Mr. Darlington relocated the family to a farm he bought near Eckville, Alberta. This investment proved to be a wise one and within a few years the farm was paid off.

When Joan reached her seventeenth birthday, she decided to leave home and look for work. She applied for a position at St. Joseph's Hospital in Edmonton. She was to receive training to become a nurse, but completed only two years before becoming ill. After her recovery, she decided not to return to the program. Her next position was as a physical therapist in Calgary, Alberta.

In 1942, Joan reported for duty with the Royal Canadian Air Force and was trained as a dental assistant. During her tour of duty, she met and married William Russell Strand, a flight engineer trainee. Upon completing his training, Strand was sent to England. By this time, Joan was pregnant and had returned home to await the birth of their baby.

She enjoyed being home, but was often disturbed by premonitions of disaster. Night after night she would dream of an airplane falling toward the earth in a ball flame. And one night, her husband appeared in a dream saying, "You know, I have been dead for ten days." Shortly after this, Joan received a telegram that Strand and all the other crew members had been killed when their plane crashed returning from a bombing mission in Germany.

Three weeks later, Russell Strand, Jr., was born. Joan remained home for another month, then decided to move to Vancouver. She stayed with her sister-in-law until she found a place of her own to buy. The house was located next door to my family. Joan and I soon became friends and on July 16, 1948, were married in Vancouver, B.C.

Two years later we immigrated to the United States. I had decided to attend Oregon State College in Corvallis.

After four years and graduation we moved again, to Nevada.

Shortly after our arrival, Joan received word of her father's death from a heart attack. It was necessary to travel over 100 miles to put Joan and the two youngest children on the train. The two older children, Russell and Dennis, stayed with me.

We left Nevada in 1955 and ended up in the country, near Bothell, Washington, after purchasing five acres of ground. The rural living provided a good environment for the children and the family raised livestock for their own use and we always had a big garden. It was about this time that Joan began writing. Within a couple of years she had sold a story to *Western Family* magazine.

It soon became apparent that Joan's health was failing. She complained of shortness of breath and dizziness and finally went to the hospital for treatment. After several days of testing and trying to diagnose the problem, she was found to be suffering from hyperglycemia, an over production of insulin by the pancreas. After ten days in the hospital and being placed on a high protein diet, she returned home to recover.

On the morning of December 6, 1961, Joan complained of terrible stomach pain. She was diagnosed with a bowel obstruction and, in critical condition, underwent emergency surgery. The surgery and other treatments proved unsuccessful, Joan's pulse gradually weakened, and she died that same day. I was devastated, but returned home to the terrible task of telling the children.

In the years following Joan's death the family stuck closely together. Eventually, I met and married a wonderful woman who cared for the children as her own, for which I have always been grateful. They are now all living worthwhile, productive lives.

Martin G. Beam
November 18, 1993
Richland, Oregon